Tiffany
Faith
Link

D0168415

Watercolor Summer

To Belinda
Blessing
No

Watercolor Summer

A NOVEL

Nan Corbitt Allen

Deep River Books
Sisters, Oregon
http://www.deepriverbooks.com

ISBN- 978-1-935265-67-2
ISBN- 10 1-935265-67-9

Library of Congress: 2011924442

Printed in the USA

Cover design by blackbirdcreative.biz

This book is dedicated...

To HIM who is able to do immeasurably more than I could ask or imagine...

To MY HUSBAND, DENNIS, who encourages me, loves me, and puts up with me...

To MY CHILDREN AND THEIR WIVES, who make me laugh, make me think, make me proud...

To MY GRANDCHILDREN, who are my heart's constant smile...

To MY GENEVA, AL FRIENDS who lived most of this time and place with me.

Prologue

The cover read, "One Moment in Time: What if you could relive it?" The magazine article was about defining moments, turning points, good and bad in life. Another attempt by pop psychologists to grate on the human race's guilt or entitlement issues. I wasn't really interested in the topic, but since sitting in airports was my least favorite thing to do, I was tempted to buy the magazine and read the article out of boredom. Fortunately, my flight was called before I had the chance.

Once on the plane, however, I did ask myself the question: which moment would I relive if I could? I knew. I wouldn't relive it because of all its sweet memories, but because it changed me forever. My one moment had to be the one in 1969, the day I met Malcolm.

Chapter One

urning thirteen wasn't as bad as I had thought. I had long imagined that on that fateful day, I would get my period, zits, and armpit hair at the same moment, perhaps at 2:37 P.M., the precise minute I had been born. But on April 25th, I only got presents and cake from my parents and a card from Mimi and Papa with a fifty-dollar bill in it. It was six weeks later when some of the dreaded symptoms of adolescence would not only begin to seize my body, but my attitude as well.

I knew something was up. Two days before summer vacation, the air was tense, more than usual, like someone had a secret they were dying to share. But my mother's moods were precarious at best and so it was impossible ever to tell what was coming next. My father, who was rarely home when she was there, was no more or less distant than usual, but I noticed that my parents' paths had so evaded each other by that time that they had fallen into sort of a vaudevillian pattern. As my father walked in the front door, my mother was conveniently going out to her art studio. When she returned, he was in his home office doing some kind of business. Though all my life my parents' connection with each other had been a little imprecise, I began to notice it more in those two days than ever before. Something was definitely about to happen.

"Kat, how would you like to go on a trip?" My mother greeted me in her usual way, curling up next to me in my bed. I opened an eye and saw that the clock read 6:15.

"Now?"

"No, silly. In a couple of days when school's out."

I was awake enough to notice there was a familiar lilt in her voice, but one I hadn't heard from her in a few months. "Where?"

I knew by then that it didn't matter where or whether I protested, I would be going to another artist colony with her soon

"I found us a place at the beach," Mama said.

I grunted and resolved not to ask where this beach might be and whether I would have an option in accompanying her. We, Mama and I, had traveled the country to who-knows-how-many states to retreat centers, artist colonies, even campsites in state parks, all with one agenda—giving my mother a new landscape to paint.

The paintings were all beautiful, and only she and I could attest to the fact that they were wonderful replicas of those swamps, valleys, mountains, seascapes. I had seen the real things and always silently admired the accuracy of her paintbrush in capturing the light, the shadows, the colors of the original. As I had gotten older, however, I had begun to notice a theme. All her paintings were studies in solitude. One tree growing in the middle of an open field. One egret standing in a thick marsh. One seagull looking out over an endless ocean as if he were wondering how far it was to the other side. The more I noticed the air of loneliness in her paintings, the more I avoided going into her studio. I would always leave that room carrying some kind of impalpable burden. So I rarely went there on my own.

There were no sad good-byes that morning. In fact, there were no good-byes at all, as usual. The day after school let out for the summer, I woke up to find Mama putting the last of the suitcases in our VW van.

"It's time to get going." She sprang into my room wearing a lavender pleated skirt, a crisp white blouse with three-quarter length sleeves, and a bright red straw hat with a floppy brim.

"Where'd you get that hat?" I sat up and tried to rake my fingers through my matted hair.

"Doesn't matter. I'll get you one when we get to Florida, babe. Now let's get going."

Florida. At least I knew a general area.

Where's Daddy? Is he going, too? I had always asked, and had come to know the answer too well. Daddy never went with us. Never that I could remember. I had guessed, for a time, that bankers somehow couldn't travel very far from their money, and for years I had passed off his absence to his need to guard the gray vaults I had seen in the center of the bank lobby. By that morning I had already resolved never to ask those two questions: Where are we going? Is Daddy going with us? They were moot. A waste of breath. And of breath, on that warm May morning, I had felt that all of mine was being sucked out as we drove away from our house.

It was impossible for me to remember all the retreats and colonies that I had been to with my mother. But sometimes she would bring out photographs of us together in a place I was sure I'd never been. She would laugh or bite her lower lip or put a name to the place.

"Oh yes. New Hampshire. The woodlands were a dream." And she'd caress the photograph as if she were trying to reconnect with its memory. "You were just learning to walk. In fact, you took your first steps there."

Those asides, those ramblings, had begun to make me extremely sad. It seemed to me, even then, that certain milestones in a child's life would have been best shared with both parents. A first step should be applauded by a proud mother and father, and so I began to feel resentful inside when my mother would mention it, as if it were the normal path of life. So many events in my life she and I had experienced together, alone…by her choice.

I was told that I had gotten my first tooth in New Mexico, and lost my first one in Maine. I had ridden my first horse in Texas, purchased my first pair of penny loafers in Pennsylvania. And I had a scar on my knee that neither my mother nor I could remember at all. The memory hadn't stuck for either of us and it became, to me, a monument to the Unknown Pain. Sometimes I would rub my finger across it, feel a twinge of sensitivity, hoping that it would conjure up some recollection of a lost day of my childhood. But it never did.

I had been hopelessly in love with my father. It sounds a little sordid now to hear myself admit it, but when I was a young child it was pure adoration. Pure. And he adored me. I was his "bee-bee" (an original ver-

sion of *baby* that he would let slide off his lower lip)
place to be in the world as a six- or seven-year-old was a
lap in my nightgown after my evening bath. I could sm
mixed with the day's oils and I would almost swoon. An
there in his lap, surrounded by the soft embrace and the soothing aroma,
that I would eventually drop off to sleep. Sometime later, I suppose, he'd
take me to my bed. Occasionally, I'd wake up when he'd brush my hair
out of my face and I would ride once again on the ecstasy of his scent.

Once I had asked my mother when I was maybe nine or ten, "What
makes Daddy smell so good?"

I remember Mama saying, "Old Spice." And then she had added
under her breath something I did not understand, but noticed that she
said with a raised brow and a sardonic smile. "Hmm, Old Spice and old
money."

"How did you and Daddy meet?" Every little girl wants to know.

It had all happened while they were in college, I was told. My
mother, who once called herself a misplaced Yankee, had arrived from
her home city of Baltimore to the University of Alabama with a full art
scholarship and a heavy dose of cynicism about the South. She told me
that she had expected plantation mansions, mammies with their hair
tied up with bandannas, slaves parching in the cotton fields, and fair-
haired coeds napping in the afternoon to avoid getting the vapors later
when they sat out on the veranda drinking their mint juleps. I had had
no idea what any of that meant, but her repartee had given me the notion
that she had found the campus to be more than she had expected. After
all, she said, she had stayed at least long enough to meet my father on a
blind date. Daddy had been an extremely handsome fraternity boy with
"a 1949 Toreador Red Chevy Street Rod to die for," Mama had said. I
could almost see it.

"Dashing. That's what he was." I had detected no cynical overtones
in that statement. I remember asking if she had liked him right off.

"Well, I thought he was handsome," she'd said. "But I really expected
him to be an arrogant rich kid."

She had been surprised at first, however, at how sweet and unaffected he was, given his parents' money and status.

My Morton grandparents, whom I called Mimi and Papa, were wealthy not just by Southern aristocracy standards, but also according to marveling local financiers. The bank my grandfather owned was just one of the many holdings he boasted in the county. There were cotton gins, grain elevators, and I later found out about some secret partner holdings he had in the liquor trade down across the Florida state line. My father, his brother, and brothers-in-law managed various parts of the business. The sum total of their worth was a point of speculation by the whole county.

"Did he like you?" I had asked Mama. I longed to know why my parents were once attracted to each other but never seemed to have a connection.

It was a rare occasion that my father would interject anything in my conversations with Mama, but once when I asked about my parents' first responses to each other, Daddy had said from behind his newspaper, "Your mama was a real looker."

My mother had smiled when he said it, but then her expression had changed. "Yes, we were really attracted to each other." And that version of the conversation had ended.

Chapter Two

E ven in the '60s, Jackson, Alabama was a place that time had neither remembered nor blessed. Its citizens seemed to have a silent pact to retain tradition regardless of how it corroded other values or kept progress at bay. Some vague status was given to certain families who owned or had once owned property in the days of Jackson's infancy. I guess it was a throwback to antebellum days. Matriarchs of these families protected the lineage, often by discouraging their children from marrying someone whose background was either questionable or untraceable. Patriarchs were less consumed with pedigree than they were with a potential suitor's connection to financial resources no matter how legal or honorable they seemed. Since I had never known my mother's parents, I wondered if Mama had had pedigree or money, but then it occurred to me that perhaps my mother had possessed neither and that was why I had the feeling that neither she nor I fit into this scene.

"Honey, your hair is almost the color of tar," Mimi said to me once when I was visiting her. She'd often comb my thick hair and drawl on with her thick accent about my features.

"Look at those pitch-black eyes, Everett," Mimi would say to my grandfather while she was holding my chin in her hand.

"Like her mother," Papa would sigh behind his newspaper. Never "like her father." And always with a sigh.

I had noticed fairly early that my features were different from everyone on my father's side. Aunts, uncles, even distant relatives. Tina, my first cousin, was a Kewpie doll complete with Shirley Temple curls and blue eyes. Ev, or Everett Morton III, her younger brother, was cherubic on the surface, but even as a toddler had a hellish temper. He was too often found taking a bite out of whatever was standing in the way of his getting what he wanted. Child, adult, dog, hamster, it didn't matter. At one time or another Little Ev had taken a chunk out of it in a fit of rage. That temperament was never discouraged, and Little Ev grew up to leave bite marks, emotionally and physically, on three wives and a couple of children. He was never legally reprimanded for any of it. The Morton name kept him out of jail and his tirades mostly out of the newspapers.

Besides "Bee-bee," my daddy called me "his raven-haired beauty." He always said it with such admiration in his voice. But whenever Mimi would refer to my raven hair, it didn't seem quite so endearing. In fact, I detected the same tone when she said it as when she would call some unfortunate peasant "jibber-jawed" or "pie-faced" or "pop-eyed." I was different, like my mother, and it was never quite in a good way.

When I was about ten years old, I began to realize that I was different not only compared to my family, but to everyone else in town.

"My mama says your mama's a hippy," a classmate named Karen told me once.

"A what?" Before that moment I'd never even heard that word.

"She smoke dope?" Another girl named Sue had chimed in.

"Y'all don't eat meat, do ya'll?" Karen added.

"I heard y'all go live in nudie colonies ever' summer."

I truly hadn't understood the comments nor the insinuations. Up until that point my mother had just been my mother, and the tensions between her, my father, and his Southern blueblood parents had just been what they were. And somehow I had managed to avoid the kind of gossip that had apparently been circulating all my life. My mother's hyphenated name, Chandler Asbury-Morton, had occasionally gotten a comment or two when she had written checks when we were out of town, but I had never been inclined to ask her about it. To me, it was the way it was, and there was nothing unusual about it at all. Karen's comment on the playground that day, however, was the moment that jump-started a new resolve in me, a resolve to keep my families' oddities to myself..

"Can you turn the radio down?" I snapped to my mother after we'd been on the road for about two hours. The first hour I had been distracted by the sack breakfast Mama had packed for us. We shared cinnamon rolls that sat in a flimsy aluminum pan wrapped in cellophane. This was a convenience food that we never bought unless we were going on a trip. There was orange juice in paper cartons and a Thermos jug full of fresh coffee.

After devouring what I could hold of breakfast, I had slumped down in the seat and tried to go back to sleep. Apparently at some time I had nodded off, only to be awakened by the Beach Boys with a rendition of "Wouldn't It Be Nice" on the radio with my mother singing backup at the top of her lungs.

"It's hot, too," I growled. Mama reached and turned up the air conditioner a notch. The cool air on my bare arms gave me goose bumps.

Mama clicked off the radio. "So, you want to tell me what's made you so grumpy this morning?"

"Are you kidding me? What do you think?"

"I would think you'd be happy we're going to Florida for the summer. I mean none of your friends are—"

"That's just it, Mama. I have friends that I won't get to see all summer long because you're dragging me off to God-knows-where...again!" I didn't really have very many close friends that I would miss, but it was ammunition I couldn't resist.

I had never challenged my mother until that moment. Every disparaging thought I'd had was buried under my breath. I had kept my attitude all inside, and I'm not sure why I chose that moment to unleash it all.

We drove in silence for the next three hours.

Chapter Three

C uss 'im."

"What?" I almost jumped out of my skin. I suppose I had been so deep in thought that I had not noticed someone come up behind me. His comment, too, had been almost unintelligible. It was more of a loud, guttural mumble.

He continued, "Unless you're a religious person, and then you might want to just turn your hat around."

I struggled to stand up on the sand and face the voice and make myself ready to run if necessary.

"What?" It was all I could say.

He stood there holding a cat, a black cat, as black as I'd ever seen. The cat hung slightly limp from the boy's arms, seemingly content to be there.

"You know when a black cat walks past you, you're s'posed to cuss 'im otherwise it's bad luck. I don't cuss, but I think if you turn your hat around it's the same thing."

The morning Florida sun was behind him, so to look into his face I had to squint and try to shade my eyes from the piercing golden glow. It didn't work. I couldn't see his face at all. I could tell, however, that he was a boy, older than me, and he was holding a docile black cat.

"I'm Malcolm," he said, stepping to his left so that I wasn't looking directly into the sun. The cat jumped out of his arms. I turned to face the boy.

My mother had often warned me about talking to strangers, and so I frantically looked around for her. I could see her up on the screened-in porch a few yards away, sipping coffee and gazing out into the gulf. I waved to make sure she could see me. She waved back. My astonishment at the boy's presence had gone and my fear was subsiding when I realized I was within reach of parental protection.

"I'm Kathleen," I said.

He nodded, as if he already knew.

"Whose cat?"

"Nobody's. Ever'body's, I guess. He walked right in front of you just now. Didn't you see 'im?"

"I guess not."

His speech was unusual. A thick Deep South accent coupled with the rasp of adolescence seemed to disguise an impediment of some sort, but I couldn't pick up on it quite yet.

"You live here?" I asked, still monitoring my mother's attention on me.

"Yeah," he said sitting down on the sand.

He wore no shoes, but he had on light gray pants and a white T-shirt that said Malcolm on the front.

"This is my shirt. It has my name on it." He rotated his trunk so I could see the big red letters across his chest.

It was becoming clear. The speech pattern, the slightly protruding lips and tongue, the short stubby fingers that lay limp beside him reminded me of another person I had known. Her name had been Rebecca, a girl a little older than I who went to the Methodist church.

When I asked once what was wrong with the girl, my mother called it Down syndrome.

"Is she retarded?" I had asked.

"Yes. She's been that way since birth. She goes to a special school, though, where they help her learn at her own rate."

Malcolm's facial features looked surprisingly like Rebecca's. In fact, their faces were almost identical. Round and pleasant. Malcolm, however, had one feature that Rebecca didn't have. His smile produced a deep dimple on his left cheek.

"How long are we staying here?" I asked one night during dinner at a seafood restaurant. We had been in Florida for exactly two days.

My mother looked up from her fried shrimp and gave me a cynical stare. "So, the girl speaks."

I dipped a hushpuppy in ketchup and then held it up as if to inspect it. "Well?"

"Not here, Kat," Mama looked around the restaurant to see if anyone was listening. No one was. Apparently, however, she was expecting me to erupt in anger.

I left the hush puppy on the plate and started to rise from my seat.

"Where are you going?" she asked.

"To the bathroom."

There were nautical accents everywhere. Netting strung from pegs with large corks intertwined. Stuffed (or maybe plastic) seagulls dangling from the ceiling, and pictures of weathered seafaring men and their vessels all along the wall. Instead of doorknobs on the restrooms there were ship's wheels. The sign on the men's room said Buoys, and the ladies' room sign said Gulls. After I got it, I rolled my eyes.

The absurdity and futility of my life at that point were crashing in on me, and they made me wish I could have a good cry. I had planned to do just that in the restroom. However, there was a line of women waiting for too few stalls, and I decided to hold it all in.

A pay phone on the wall nearby gave me an idea. Digging into my pocket, I silently prayed that I'd have a dime that I'd somehow forgotten about. I didn't. But the plan that I was conjuring up put the tears on hold for a while.

Chapter Four

What stinks?"

I'm not sure if I actually said it out loud, but that was the senti-ment screaming from my brain as I woke up on the one-week anniversary of our Florida excursion. The aroma was putrid, like rotting food, and before I left my bed and started my railings about it, I checked my own surroundings to make sure it was not emanating from me. It wasn't.

"Hey, babe." Mama turned from her easel as I entered the porch. "You slept the clock around."

"What is that horrible smell?" I complained in a morning growl.

"And the top o' the mornin' to you, too, lassie."

I usually laughed at her faux Irish accent, but I was determined not to this time. "No, really. What is that smell?"

"I'm told it's the paper mill."

"The paper mill?"

"Yes, Jeanette says that when the wind is just right, the aroma of the mills in Panama City and Port St. Joe converge here. Add the smell of the saltwater to the humid air, and the smell is...well...strong."

Mama had already turned back to her work and was dabbing at it with her brush as she spoke. I looked over her shoulder out of habitual curiosity and, as always, was stunned by her work. The paper that had been blank just days before was giving birth now to a seascape I could swear was more magnificent than the original. The clouds over the gulf were slightly pouty, not heavy with rain, but dense enough to block the yellow sun and cast a grayish haze over the calm surf. I did not want to be distracted from my own pout, so I tried to shake off the marvel at my mother's work and continue sulking.

"It makes my eyes burn!" I wiped at my sleep-swollen eyes in an effort to gain pity and to build my case that I was miserable.

"Well, that's the sulfur in the smoke from the mill, Jeanette says, and it's totally harmless." I was disappointed that she didn't turn around to witness my suffering. Instead, she continued making the sky magically emerge from the painting. "There's juice in the fridge, and Jeanette said she'd make a hot breakfast for you when you got up. Or there's cereal in the cupboard."

I didn't acknowledge. I did look at the clock, and at 11:15, I realized it was way past breakfast time. I guessed, however, that no matter what time it was, the first meal of the day could possibly be called breakfast.

I chased the last Frosted Flakes in my bowl quickly, disliking nothing more than cereal that had sat in milk too long and gotten limp.

Sulfur.

Then I remembered why the smell was familiar. In science class the semester before, Mr. Bowman, our teacher had exposed us to this element by letting us sniff it in its acid form.

"Waft it, students. Just waft it," he'd said, passing a beaker of the liquid and warning us not to let the pungent smell get too close to our nasal cavities.

"It is very strong and could damage the tender membranes of your nose. So just pass it quickly in front of you. That's what I mean by wafting, students."

Mr. Bowman took seventh-grade science seriously, having a reputation among students of being severe and among the parents as being thorough.

The smell of the sulfuric acid had haunted me all day. I had mentioned to Karen at lunch that everything I smelled, including the cafeteria food, smelled like the acid.

"You probably damaged your membranes, then. You didn't waft it. You smelled it!" And I worried for a week about my membranes. I finally forgot all about it when the aroma memory faded.

But there, as I stared into my empty cereal bowl, the memory came back with the addition of Mr. Bowman's lecture that day.

"Sulfur was once called brimstone by the ancients. It is referred to in Scripture." A word he always pronounced, "scrip-chah." Mr. Bowman, who made no apologies for it, often lapsed into a sermonic style of teaching, for he was also the pastor of the only black church in Jackson. The black students in the school who attended Mr. Bowman's church testified to the rest of us that he was as vibrant and animated in the pulpit as he was in the classroom.

"Genesis 19:24. Then the Lord rained upon Sodom and upon Gomorrah brimstone and fire from the Lord out of heaven," he began from memory.

There had been a single *hallelujah* from the back of the room and a few giggles from the front.

"Revelation says that those without the Lord will be cast into hell which is a lake of fire burning with brimstone!"

I could see the fire stoking just behind my teacher's eyes. He was obviously being swept away into what was a recurring charismatic frenzy. I had seen it several times before, especially when he'd talked about the world and its origin.

"If Mr. Darwin were here right now, I would tell him that his so-called 'mystery of mysteries' is not found in his theory of evolution. His book *On the Origin of Species* will not survive ten thousand years as the Holy Scrip-chahs have because it is not Truth. For the origin of man is not from primordial ooze, but from the hand of Almighty God-d." The *d* on God was always over-enunciated.

I got chills sometimes when Mr. Bowman would start preaching, for I was convinced that no one with that much conviction in his voice could be speaking anything but the truth.

Suddenly however, on Sulfur Day, the teacher had caught himself before he went too far and before we tuned out his lesson plan, which often was seriously delayed by such journeys into his true passion of preaching.

"Hell. That's what this is," I mumbled into the last bit of orange juice in my glass. And I was a little self-satisfied that I had at least defined my situation and even more that I had gotten away with saying a naughty word out loud.

Chapter Five

You're just sorry! That's what you are. Sorry as gully dirt!"
I more than recognized the grating voice of Jeanette Hudspeth, man-
ager of the artist colony, unofficial guardian of Malcolm, and "chief,
cook, and bottle-washer," as she often referred to herself. But the anger
and revulsion in her voice, as if she were berating the absolute scum of
the earth, startled me. Admittedly Jeanette was annoying in every way
that a thirteen-year-old girl could imagine, but her language was hardly
ever harsh or unkind. Especially when it came to Malcolm. Her words to
and about her teenage charge could be strict and direct at times, but
always were punctuated with a hug and her favorite endearment. Precious. She could shake her arthritic finger at a naughty mess of dishes or
dirty clothes that Malcolm had left and then turn and grab him in a full
embrace and backslap and say, "But I love you anyway, precious." I'd seen
it before and witnessed the burden of guilt on Malcolm's face fade into
repentance and then to determination to fix whatever mess he was guilty
of. I had never heard Jeanette call him or anyone an unkind name.

I hung back onto the screened-in porch just off the kitchen to hear
who she was talking to, and to keep safe distance in case the woman had
snapped and was shooting insults and cooking utensils at anyone in her
path.

Jeanette moved to the stove and gave the pot of butter beans a look
and a stir, all the while muttering, "Sorry. Sorry. Sorry!" I pressed my
body up against the door frame to hide, but also to keep listening.

"Who does she think she's foolin'? Not me, that's for sure.
Trash...gully dirt!"

I was hearing it but not believing it—until I recognized the Dreft
detergent commercial in the background. Ah yes, the time was right, at

lunch preparation time, when Jeanette tuned into her favorite soap opera, *As the World Turns*. Jeanette was addicted to the goings-on in Oakdale, and I reckoned the media vixen Lisa Hughes was up to another one of her manipulative schemes. I had only watched the show a few times myself and had to admit that Lisa had an evil way about her. Her smirk and smile ended many episodes. And, I'm sorry to admit, I grew to admire her devilish exploits. Lisa usually got what she wanted and then walked away looking innocent as a lamb.

"What's for lunch, Jeanette?" Her body jolted. I'd startled her, not so much by my sudden appearance in the kitchen, but by my uncharacteristic chipper approach.

"Uh, butter beans, collard greens, hoe cake, pork chops…"

"Sounds good."

Jeanette was suddenly quiet, which was a rare occurrence in the three weeks I had known her. If Jeanette wasn't talking back to the soap opera characters, she was talking to herself in lists of ingredients she needed for the current recipe, or she was telling Malcolm what chore would be next on his agenda. Jeanette believed that Malcolm's mental state did not affect his ability to carry out physical tasks, although I think she knew that his physical state was somewhat fragile as well.

I was guessing that my sudden turn at that moment was a great puzzle to Jeanette and she was dumbfounded to speechlessness. Well, I had heard her use the phrase "You'll draw more bees with honey than with vinegar." I was getting smart enough to know exactly what that meant and how to use it to my advantage.

"Letter came for yo' mama," Jeanette finally spoke. "Don't know who it's from or nuthin'. Don't read other people's mail."

I turned on my heels and faced Jeanette. "Where is it?"

"I give it to yo' mama. It was addressed to her."

I knew where to find Mama. My mother could always be found in one of two places: in the studio on the porch that overlooked the gulf where other artists had set up their canvases, or a few hundred yards away set up on the bayside. Though I did not want to appear so, I had been watching for weeks in awe at my mother's latest painting. The subtle ripples of the bay at dawn were a backdrop for the true subjects of her masterpiece. Two crabs sitting in a homemade trap, looking out with languid eyes. As I watched the crabs come to life with each brushstroke, I noticed they became hopeless, then desperate, then dead. What was Mama saying in the painting? She always said something, or at least she pretended to. She said that the white flowers she had painted once, on the rocky hillsides of Colorado represented life and purity springing forth in spite of their hostile environment. She said a few sky pictures she had painted meant newness, or freedom, or peace, or frustration. I almost believed the analysis of her work, but I had had a dose of cynicism for a long time about my mother's depth. I had never believed she could feel such profound things. I later found out how wrong I was.

"Mama?" She wasn't at her usual place on the porch. The stool sat empty and the canvas looked recently untouched. I passed through the kitchen and out the carport door. I crossed the road and looked out toward the bay. I didn't see her there.

"Mama?" I called. Back through the house. I made a quick search of the rooms off the kitchen. The doors to our bedroom and bathroom were open, and I saw no one. Jeanette was stirring something on the stove with one hand while keeping her gaze on the TV.

I ended up back on the porch, put my hands on my hips, and silently chided my mother for disappearing like that. Then I noticed footprints in the powder sand leading away from the cabin. I scanned the shoreline and saw Malcolm picking up seashells and putting them in a plastic bucket. I didn't want to go out there. I wasn't in the mood to talk to him right then. But I needed to find my mother and find out if it was my father who had written her this letter.

Quietly I opened the screen door, trying to not draw Malcolm's attention. I slipped off my flip-flops, which would only bog down my passage through the sand, and headed in the opposite direction from Malcolm. He didn't notice me.

At midday the top of the sand was already scorching, and the only relief I could muster was by walking heavy-footed so that my feet plunged past the hot surface to the cooler sand below.

The footprints climbed up a small dune and disappeared among the sea oats. I followed, hoping it was Mama and not one of the other two artists at the colony, both whom I had tried to avoid, not wanting to get sucked into their life stories and how and why they'd come to paint. I just wanted to find my mother, and most importantly, see who the letter was from.

There Mama was sitting on the sand dune amid the sea oats, completely engrossed in the letter. I hated to disturb her, so I stood quietly for a moment. Looking at my Mama was something I had done a lot in my life. Just looking at her. She was exquisite. It was hard to take my eyes off her. Her jet-black hair was long and shimmering, past her shoulders but swept up in a ponytail. Her skin and eyes were like toffee, and her soft face included beautiful full lips. Lithe, but not bony, her body moved like a dancer. I could see how Daddy would be attracted to her, or how any other man would, too. With that thought coming to my mind, I had a sudden fear that the letter Mama held in her hand was not from my father. What if this was from another man? A lover? The thought had only casually crossed my mind a few times in my thirteen years, but this time it became a serious thought. I didn't want to know this side of her. I didn't want to think of how this would hurt Daddy. I didn't want to think that this might be a very true thought.

As I turned to descend the dune, the sand squeaked under my feet, and this time Mama looked up from the letter.

"Hey, baby. Got a letter from home. Here, Daddy wrote one especially to you…and I think there's something green and folded inside yours." She said it like a taunt she used to use on me when I was five and wouldn't finish my vegetables. "There's a treat for somebody who takes two more bites of green beans," she'd say. But right then I didn't care about the taunt, I lunged for the letter. It was indeed addressed to me. It was in a separate envelope, unopened, which made me wonder how Mama knew that Daddy had sent me some money.

Knowing there was cash inside made me open the letter slower than I wanted to. I didn't want the five-dollar bill to go flying off into the gulf. I carefully pulled out the two-page letter, which, to my surprise, had a ten-dollar-bill folded inside it. I shoved the bill in the pocket of my cut-offs and clumsily opened the letter.

"Dear Bee-bee,"

It was from Daddy! I looked around to tell somebody that fact, but Mama already knew it, and there was no one else in sight. I read the greeting two more times and was about to go on reading when out of nowhere Malcolm appeared behind me.

"Kat."

I jerked my head around.

"Malcolm! What are you doing here? You nearly scared me to death."

"Sorry, Kat. But Miss Jeanette says it's time for lunch."

"Oh, Mama. Did you hear? Jeanette wants us for lunch."

Mama nodded, but her eyes were still glued to the letter.

Malcolm walked about four steps in front of me down the dune. I could tell Mama was following behind me about the same distance.

"Dear Bee-bee..." I read out loud. "Hey, Malcolm, this is a letter to me from my Daddy."

Malcolm stopped and looked back. His smile had genuine joy in it for me, and he held up one stubby thumb.

Chapter Six

It took almost a month before I learned Malcolm's story. I hadn't tried very hard to find out why he was at the colony and what his relationship to Jeanette was. I knew that Jeanette was not his mother or even a blood relative, but past that I hadn't really cared. I had mostly been obsessed with how I could get out of there. But one sleepless, humid night I heard Mama and Jeanette talking on the back porch. That night I found out all about dear Malcolm.

"The daddy looked funny out of his eyes from the get-go, you know. The mama looked kindly, like a whipped puppy, lots of the time."

I could only see their silhouettes. Mama's body was turned sideways in the rocking chair toward Jeanette, and I could tell she was listening intently. Each of the ladies held a coffee mug.

"Was it the man or the woman who was the artist?" Mama asked.

"That's what was so odd. Neither of 'em painted nary a thing while they were here. They paid their room and board, so I didn't bother 'em. Just cooked for 'em and for little Malcolm like I was s'posed to. Thought maybe they was waitin' for inspiration like some of you painters do. They was only here a few days 'fore they left."

"How old was Malcolm then?"

"Don't rightly know. I'm guessing that he was five or six. After I took 'im in, I wanted to git 'im in a special program that the county school was offering. I needed a birth certificate for 'im. My friend Gladys who works down at the county office tried to look him up in their files, but couldn't find nuthin' on him in Florida. She called around a little bit to other states, but didn't find no record of birth. Could be, I guess, there never was a record of his birth. Like he didn't exist or something."

Jeanette's voice trailed off for a few seconds.

"Gladys really helped us out though she wasn't really s'posed to do it. She created a birth certificate with just the information we knew. I had the parents' names, but I figured they didn't want 'im anyways, so I told Gladys to give 'im my last name. Hudspeth. We picked a birth date... August 20, which was the day the daddy and the mama left him here, and Gladys made me a copy so's I'd have something to take to the school.

"So, the parents just walked away and left him here?" Mama asked.

"Yeah. Said they was going out to a club one night, asked if I'd look after him. I said sure. He wasn't no trouble at all. Sweetest thing what ever lived, that boy. But they never came back. Days went by and I didn't hear a peep. I figured they'd at least leave word where their people lived, you know, so's he could go live with a grandmother or aunt or somethin'. But I never heard another word."

I couldn't believe what I was hearing. Did Jeanette mean that Malcolm had been abandoned at the colony?

"Did you ever try to find the parents? Did you call the police?"

Jeanette was silent for what seemed like five minutes or so. I could see Mama look over at her; I thought maybe she was checking to see if Jeanette had nodded off.

"No," Jeanette finally answered before taking a sip from her coffee cup.

"Think they're...dead...maybe?"

"Don't know."

Mama reached over and touched Jeanette's fleshy bare arm as though she understood far more than Jeanette had communicated.

"I pray ever' night that those people won't come back here. I know it's wrong to pray like that, but they didn't love that boy. Fact, they was embarrassed by 'im and treated 'im real bad. I never heard such talk like that."

"What do you mean?"

"Well, I ain't no saint myself, but I believe all God's creatures, even...ones like Malcolm...got some purpose and all need to be loved. You know, I heard that daddy call that boy the village idiot and a Mongoloid, and said stuff like 'He ain't got sense enough to get out of a shower o' rain. Malcolm would cry when his daddy would talk mean like that, which was most of the time, and the boy would come runnin' to me and wrap those chubby arms around my neck and..."

Mama leaned over and pulled Jeanette into a gentle hug. I could tell that Jeanette was choking back sobs.

After a few cleansing breaths, Jeanette continued.

"Malcolm used to ask me 'bout his mama and daddy and when was they comin' to get him. I'd tell him real soon, that they were on a trip or somethin', but I knew they wasn't coming back. And ever' day that went by, I hoped more and more that they wouldn't."

"Malcolm's just become yours, then."

"Yeah, never had chur'n of my own and so I just felt like Malcolm was a gift. A gift straight outta heaven. I knew he would need special care, but he was mine, and I thanked the Lord for sending 'im to me." Jeanette's voice quivered slightly.

"You love him as a son, just as I love my daughter."

Mama's voice had so much compassion in it that I began to cry. I wasn't sure if the tears were pity for Malcolm, for Jeanette, or for me. I suppose that Malcolm deserved them more than any of us at that point.

The rain on the tin roof was both deafening and soothing, and after I established where I was and that it was morning again, I closed my eyes and must have slept another two hours. At some point the rain stopped, and the next sound I remember hearing was like fingernails on a chalkboard. Scraping, then growling, then scraping again.

I didn't bother to put on shorts or a bathrobe. I crawled out of bed wearing Daddy's old T-shirt and followed the sound.

Mama was nowhere to be found. Jeanette was standing in front of the open refrigerator. I couldn't see her head, but the rest of her large muumuu-clad body was quite recognizable poking out from behind the refrigerator door.

I heard the sound again. Scraping, growling, scraping. All I could figure was that the refrigerator was on the blink, and Jeanette was somehow trying to fix it. Suddenly Jeanette stood up with a glass bottle of milk in one hand and a pitcher of fresh-squeezed orange juice in the other. She kicked the refrigerator door shut with her stovepipe-shaped leg. The sound followed her all the way to the kitchen table. That racket was coming out of her nasal passages! I watched in awe as this woman walked across the room emanating the most hideous sounds I'd ever heard come out of a human body. Scraping, growling, scraping, growling. "In" was definitely scraping, a noise only made possible by the violent vibration of the soft palate in her throat. The "out" growling was like a fierce bubbly snore. I looked around to see if anyone else was around to hear it and was as transfixed as I. No one was there. I was the only witness.

"What in the world?"

"Hey, shug, your Mama went to the store for me this morning. I've got the science problems something awful today. Must be the rain. Mold. I'm allergic to mold, and rain makes the mold worse. Last time we had a real gully washer, I guess was a couple of months ago, and my sciences got so swole that I near 'bout died."

Sciences. Did she mean sinuses?

"Anyway, the time before that I got the allergy all the way down in my bronicals."

Bronchia, maybe?

I turned and left the scene without her ever noticing I was gone. I slipped back into bed and slept another hour only to dream about my seventh-grade science teacher, Mr. Bowman. He was teaching us about the respiratory tract and showing transparencies on an overhead projector. There were the trachea, the lungs, the alveolar ducts...the bronicals. Oh, no! It was definitely time to get up for the day.

The box said "Kat," written in Mama's handwriting. It hadn't been in plain view exactly, but since the box was sitting in my closet, I was sure it was not off limits, so I opened it.

Mrs. Beasley was lying on top of the pile. I lifted her out of the box. First, I smiled. Then I winced and rolled my eyes.

What had Mama done? Obviously, she had packed some of my things. Toys. But it had only been maybe two Christmases ago that I had gotten Mrs. Beasley. Of course, back then my favorite TV show had been *Family Affair*. Each week I watched orphaned twins Buffy and Jody and their teenaged sister, Cissy, live through conflict and crisis with their bachelor uncle in New York City. The resident sage in the series was Mr. French, Uncle Bill's butler, who usually ended up stating the obvious and calling the family to a group hug at the end. But Mrs. Beasley was the true rock in it all. She was Buffy's doll and was a most excellent listener when the freckle-faced girl would cry sad tears. Every little girl in America, including me, got Mrs. Beasley dolls for Christmas. She sat on my bed every day. But after a while, I found out she wasn't that great a listener after all. Or maybe I hadn't really given her a fair chance.

I was most excited to find my record player in the bottom of the box. Since we got the hi-fi in the living room, I hadn't really used my little record player that often. So, had Mama remembered the 45s? Yes. Fifth Dimension, Tommy James and the Shondells, the Rascals. I knew every word and note of each record, including the background vocals, and when I had listened to and sung each song at least ten times that day, I felt better than I had since I had arrived at the colony.

Chapter Seven

"Wwhat are you doing, Kath-a-leen?" Malcolm had started calling me by my full first name. I asked him why, and he smiled and kind of blushed and said, "It's a pretty name. I like it better than Kat."

I tried to not look annoyed at the interruption, but I was trying hard to put my thoughts into words on a page.

"Writing a letter, Malcolm."

"A letter to your dad?"

I nodded, desperately trying to remember my train of thought.

"I can write. I can read, too."

I put my pencil and paper down. The words were gone, the mood broken. I was hoping Malcolm would realize he was keeping me from an essential task.

"Want me to write my name for you, Kath-a-leen?"

"Malcolm…" I tried to grab my paper and pencil and hide it under my leg, but it was too late. Malcolm had already taken the tablet, flipped over to a blank page, and started scrawling his name with his awkward grip on the pencil. His enlarged tongue protruded even farther than usual as he concentrated on his writing.

Mama had told me that Malcolm was in public school in a special education program at Bay High School. That's why I had believed him when he told me he went to high school, but Mama also told me Malcolm was at about a third-grade level as far as his basic skills. His IQ was around 70, she said.

"There. That's my name." Malcolm turned the tablet back to me.

"Good. Malcolm. Good." I tried to cover my sarcasm. His signature did look somewhat childish, but it was very neat and a little artistic. "Very good," I added. Malcolm smiled so wide that when his dimple appeared, it made me catch my breath. Then he turned and walked away.

I flipped the pages back to where I had left off. I thought for a moment and then continued.

> Daddy, this boy named Malcolm who lives here is really
> creepy, and I don't feel comfortable around him. That, and
> all the reasons I gave you before, makes me plead with you
> to come and take me home.
> Please, Daddy. I love you. I miss you.
> Sincerely,
> Bee-bee

It was overly dramatic, even for me. But words like *plead* were not too sophisticated for me, were they? I was thirteen, after all, and I had a pretty extensive vocabulary, but the thing that bothered me most about my letter was how I had embellished the truth about the cabin. Even though the place was a little older, it was immaculate. The plumbing was all working, the air conditioner window units were fully functional, and the food was delicious. All this was contrary to my accounts to Daddy.

And Malcolm, he was not as I had reported at all. My guilt for telling such lies almost kept me from mailing the letter.

'm not sure when it happened, but my arms and legs had gotten so long that they almost completely wrapped around Daddy's waist. The moment I saw him standing at the door of my room, I ran and jumped up on him just as I had done as a five-year-old. And just as he had done then, he shifted my body to his hip so that I was off center and, I guess, easier to carry. I realized then that my feet were only a few inches off the ground. I had been so surprised and so glad to see him that I would not let go of him even though I knew it was hard for him to bear the weight of my almost-grown body.

"Hot buns," he would say when he bumped my backside on the water heater as he carried me to the breakfast table each morning since I could remember. It was one of the many silly daddy-daughter rituals we had developed, and though I sometimes acted as though I was tired of them, I never really was.

"Why, look at you. You're brown as a bean," Daddy said as he still tried to juggle my lanky body on his hip.

"I've been out in the sun a lot. Why didn't you tell me you were coming down here, Daddy?"

"Well, I didn't know myself until this morning. Just got in the car and started driving. Figured it being Fourth of July holiday, I could stand to be away for a couple of days to see my favorite daughter," he teased.

"Oh, Daddy. I'm your only daughter." I loosened my grip around his neck, and my feet found the floor. "Does Mama know you're here?"

"I guess not. I looked for her when I drove up. There was nobody around, so I knocked on the door. Didn't you hear me?"

I shook my head.

"I just walked in, and there you were." I put my feet on the floor.

Holding me out at arm's length, he added, "And you've grown two inches since May."

"Yeah, up and down, but nothing out front," I said dejectedly, remembering my shapeless body.

"Oh, don't worry 'bout that. You'll get that soon enough…too soon, I'm afraid." Now Daddy sounded slightly distant.

"Don't you turn around, mister. I've got a big ol' heavy black skillet aimed right at your head."

I looked beyond my father to see Jeanette standing there holding an iron skillet in one hand and a carving knife in the other. Her lumpy body was cocked and ready to put some hurt on this intruder.

Before Daddy could even turn around and look behind him, I jumped between them. "Jeanette, this is my daddy. Put those weapons down," I demanded like Danno in *Hawaii Five-0*. Jeanette did not comply immediately, however.

Daddy whipped around with a genuine smile. "Jeanette? Finally, we meet. I've heard so much about you. George Morton." He extended his hand, and Jeanette slowly laid the skillet and knife down, wiped her chubby hand on her apron, and connected it with my father's open palm.

"Pleased to meet you, Mr. Morton." I'd never seen Jeanette blush before, but it was obvious she was charmed and as overwhelmed by my daddy's appearance as I was. He often had that effect on people, especially members of the opposite sex. His thick, blond hair crowned his too-pale face, but that just made his blue eyes pierce you even more. His features were the antithesis of my mother's, but were just as striking.

"George?" Mama entered the room.

"Chan." My parents went quickly to each other, but I noticed that their embrace was just a tiny bit tentative. Familiar, yet uncomfortable.

"I'll leave y'all alone then. But I'll set another plate at the dinner table." Jeanette's voice faded, as did her presence from the room.

I couldn't leave them. I just couldn't. It was like I was paralyzed, or hoping to paralyze that moment. My parents together in the same house!

It had been weeks since I had seen that. I wanted to paint this picture forever in my mind. I was ecstatic to see my father and mother together, or
maybe I was afraid, afraid that this moment would disappear too soon.
I started to cry. Yes, I was afraid of the truth, of the inevitable. And suddenly I hated growing up.

I was caught in a lie, but I was sure it was worth it.

"George, I'm not sure why Kat told you that about Malcolm. He's
the sweetest thing…"

I immediately squatted behind the kitchen cabinet. I'm not certain
why. Perhaps it was an attempt to hide. However, I was already hiding,
sneaking out of bed after my parents were sure I was asleep so that I
could listen to their conversation on the porch.

My letters to Daddy had been dramatic, heart-rending, passion-
ate…lies. Mostly. I was honest about missing home, missing him, and
about my misery, but I had simply made up things about Malcolm that
I knew would draw my father in and perhaps force him to take me away
from that place.

"That little devil." I didn't detect any anger in my father's voice. That
meant that he hadn't taken my pleas to go home seriously. I feared that
more than I dreaded his anger.

Chapter Nine

like your dad."

I didn't have to look to know it was Malcolm standing on the dune behind me. He had been watching me watch the gulf for, I guessed, three minutes.

"He's very nice," Malcolm finally said when I didn't respond to his first comment.

"What do you want, Malcolm?" I said, trying for a sullen mumble rather than a biting admonishment. I'm not sure I succeeded.

"Nothing."

If Jeanette or Mama had sent Malcolm to get me for a meal or a trip to the store, he would have told me. The fact that Malcolm said, "Nothing," made me sure that he was sensing my melancholy again and wanted to help.

"Can I sit down?"

I was surprised at Malcolm's boldness. Until now, each time he had tried to make conversation or to help me in the midst of my moods, he had simply taken my silence as his cue to exit. Today was different.

Daddy had been at the colony for three days and until a few moments before, I had stuck to him like glue. I had snuggled next to him at every meal, walked with him on the beach, sat on his lap, my legs hanging over the chair arm. That morning at breakfast, my father had casually talked about his trip home. Is there a better route? Should he go through Andalusia and visit Aunt Lucille in the nursing home? He was so matter-of-fact about his leaving, as if it was never under discussion, that I was totally caught off guard.

"You're leaving?" Before anyone could answer, I added, "When?" And before Daddy could answer that, I threw my fork onto my plate and ran out of the kitchen, through the porch, and tried to slam the screened door as I exited. I looked back to see that the wind had caught the door and kept it from slamming. It made me even angrier that my tantrum had not made its intended impact. I stomped up to my adopted dune and sat down hard, fantasizing how Daddy would surely come running after me and either vow to stay at the colony or apologize because he had failed to tell me that he was actually taking me back with him.

Instead, I sat in the sand with Malcolm sitting next to me, waiting for me to pour out my woes to him.

That's when the tears came. First mine, then Malcolm's.

"I wish I had a hand-che-cuff," he said after several minutes. With compound words, Malcolm had learned to sound them out slowly. But his attempt to say *handkerchief* was also a mispronunciation he had learned from Jeanette. So many of Jeanette's words and phrases were either jumbled or rearranged that they almost became comical. Mama loved the color of these Jeanette-isms, as she called them. They irritated me immensely. I had even called Jeanette ignorant, not to her face, but mumbled under my breath each time she'd say something like, *wonst* instead of *once*, *sim-u-lar* instead of *similar*, *demader* for *tomato*, and especially the made-up words; when her cake failed to rise in the oven, she had declared it flat as a flitter. Add to these the episode about sciences and bronicals, and my annoyance with her, the place, my world, was about to go from minor miff to full outrage.

I turned to sharply correct Malcolm about the handkerchief mispronunciation, but something stopped me. When I actually looked at Malcolm I could see that his tears were real and his heart was broken. For me. It was the first time I had actually looked at Malcolm that way. No, it was the first time I had looked at Malcolm at all. His pudgy face had been quite visible at every meal, at almost every minute of my days there, but I had never really looked at him. The dimple on his smiling cheek that I had noticed at our first meeting I had forgotten so soon, though I'm sure it had shown itself many times. Malcolm smiled a lot. He laughed a lot, too, especially while watching Popeye cartoons in the afternoon. Something about Popeye's yucking laugh made Malcolm laugh, too. On the back end of Malcolm's laugh there was always a lame attempt at imitating Popeye's. It annoyed me and I had vowed to make myself scarce at cartoon hour.

At that moment, however, I wanted to hear the Popeye laugh. I wanted to see the smile dimple instead of seeing the tears run down his face and hear the occasional "Oh boy" that Malcolm would sigh after a deep breath.

My fear and my anger were overshadowed at that moment by my shame. A car door slammed, and an engine started, then revved for a few seconds. Gravel popped and ground underneath the tires. The roar of the automobile disappeared slowly in the distance.

That was it. That was my good-bye.

Chapter Ten

I don't know why I hadn't seen it before. I had walked the beach in both directions for miles, it seemed, but my discovery of the Hangout happened when I heard the music that seemed to call me to it.

I knew the song. "Chain of Fools." It had been an Aretha Franklin hit on WPAP and every time I heard it, I started to dance. I never really listened to the words, though, until that moment.

Finally, somebody understood. Aretha. No one had put it into words for me before, but suddenly I knew who I was. I was a pawn. I was a fool.

I had pretended not to care when my mother told me that morning. I said I understood. I said I wasn't upset. I said I would be fine.

"Your father and I are legally separating," Mama had said. I wasn't surprised to hear it, but I was surprised that my parents had made that decision during the three short days my father had visited us in Florida. I had been by his side almost constantly, so when had they had a chance to talk about this?

"He wanted to tell you this himself, while he was here, but it never seemed the right time." So, had I been invisible? Had he not sensed my presence all day, every day?

"He did leave you a note though." A note? It doesn't even classify as a letter? It's a note? I had passed notes in history class with a sentence or two about how cute Roy Fowler was. Those notes had said nothing of importance. And this was my father's way of saying he was leaving us?

"Now Kat, understand that Daddy's not leaving us. I'm not leaving him." Then what? Am I the one leaving? Not a bad idea.

"We'll be going back to Jackson in a few weeks and then we'll talk more." About what? About leaving again? About moving to another state? About divorce?

I had been silent during Mama's speech. What had there been to say? My cool attitude to the announcement apparently gave my mother the impression that I was okay with it all. Within the next few minutes she had returned to her bayside nest with tubes of oil paints, canvas, and palette in hand.

I crammed the note into my shorts pocket and walked out the porch door and headed westward down the beach.

"Hey." A voice from behind me startled me as I leaned against a post to the entrance to the open-air dance hall.

I almost expected to turn around and find Malcolm there, but I found that the greeting had come from a boy about Malcolm's age, but very different from Malcolm. This boy was tall and blond and perfectly tanned. His white teeth stood out like sunbeams against his brown face, and his smile seemed to be never ending.

"I'm Barry," he said. I froze. I must have been in a semi-catatonic state, and so Barry shrugged and walked through the middle of the dance hall and toward the concession stand. As he walked away, I noticed the whistle around his neck swing side to side across his chest.

Ed's Beach Service. That's what it said on the back of his T-shirt.

A lifeguard? I had met an actual lifeguard on the beach? Every Beach Boys song came flooding to my mind. "Surfer Girl." "Good Vibrations."

The swoon lasted only a minute or two before I looked down at my oversized feet and then to my shapeless, long legs. I drew my arms into my chest, suddenly aware of my undeveloped thirteen-year-old body. I raked my hands through my hair as alarms went off in my head. I was a child. At least I looked like one. And as two shapely, blonde, bikini-clad girls walked toward me with a pair of handsome bronzed boys following, I turned and broke into a jog back down the beach.

I hadn't hidden the box in the closet to keep anyone from stealing its contents mostly because there wasn't much of value in it. Though I was unhappy in my surroundings, I never suspected the people around me of being thieves. My hiding the shoebox full of my stuff was mostly so that I could say that there was something that was totally mine. A tiny door at the back of the closet that had a piece of wood nailed to the sheetrock next to it was crude, but a sufficient latch nonetheless to hold the door shut. Once I had started to ask Jeanette why the door was there at all, but just on the outside chance she'd never noticed it, I decided to pretend it was my own little secret.

I had exactly fifty-seven dollars in the flimsy leather wallet. The wallet had been Daddy's. A few years before, when he got a new one, he had let me have this one. I loved to smell it. The genuine leather smell mixed with the scent of Old Spice and time was so sweet and comforting. Right then, however, I did not want to be comforted, especially not by my father's rejects. I just ripped out the bills I had left from birthday gifts, money sent by my grandparents and Daddy through the mail, and a few dollars Mama had given me as mad money, and headed to the front door that opened to the highway.

Chapter Eleven

C an I help you?" the girl asked me at the drugstore.
"Uh, I'm just looking, thank you." And then I saw it on the shelf with all the other hair-coloring products.

Sun-In. I didn't even read the label. I just knew that this was an inexpensive and subtle way to lighten my hair and make myself look like those blond bikini girls. Well, there were other things, but I had some money to spend at the swimsuit shop and rolls of toilet tissue if I needed it.

I was happy to find that swimsuits were on sale. It being the middle of summer, I guessed the demand was less than at the beginning. Even I had all the swimsuits I would need, or at least all my mother thought I'd need.

"No, honey. We need to stick to one-pieces for you. At least for a few more years." I hadn't argued, because I knew she was right. The green pull-on suit with the dotted Swiss ruffles around the neck and around the hips did fill me out more, but the ruffles looked so childish. Especially in the water. The ruffles flounced and floated in the gulf, and I was glad that I was usually alone when I swam.

One thing that hadn't occurred to me was the difference I'd have in the tan lines. Even under my suit I was always dark, but the sun had just made me like Daddy said, brown as a bean. Every two-piece I tried on was laughable. A dark arc extended down my back, but my front was three shades lighter than the rest of me. It would take a week or more of sun exposure to make me the same color all over. I wouldn't quit, though, until I found a two-piece that worked.

Finally. Perfect. It was blue denim with white topstitching, padded on the top, which linked to the bottom in the front by a metal buckle.

Yeah, it was sophisticated, mature, and not too much of anything. But my challenge was to get it into the house, wear it on the beach to tan out the lines, and get up the nerve to wear it to the Hangout.

And I needed to lighten my hair, of course. So to speed up the process I added some lemon juice and hydrogen peroxide to my Sun-In bottle.

"Kath-a-leen, what is wrong with your hair?" Malcolm was the first to notice it two days later, even before I discovered it.

"What? What do you mean?"

"It's orange."

"It is not." I closed my eyes again and lay back on the beach chair I had dragged up to the dune. I was sure Malcolm was wrong or was kidding me. However, I never remembered a time since I'd known him that Malcolm had either been wrong or teasing.

"Okay."

I thought he had gone.

After a few seconds, he asked, "What is this?" I opened one eye to see Malcolm standing over me holding my Sun-In bottle in his hand.

"That is none of your business, Malcolm. It's…girl stuff, and you shouldn't touch it. And don't tell Mama or Jeanette either, because—"

"Sun-In," Malcolm read. "I saw this on TV. It makes your hair light."

By that time, I was sitting up and pulling the ends of my hair around to inspect it with one hand. With the other hand I was reaching for the spray bottle, which Malcolm quickly surrendered.

"Why do you want to make your hair light, Kath-a-leen?" Malcolm had a way of cutting to the chase.

"I just do, Malcolm. Now don't tell anybody."

"I won't." He shook his head and waved his hands to show me he was truly trying to dismiss the whole scene.

In the six weeks I had been there, I had not confided in anyone my true feelings. I had poured out my heart in letters to my father, but most of that had been melodrama for the sake of gaining attention. One thing I had learned, however, was that if I did choose to share my thoughts with someone, I could most definitely entrust them to Malcolm.

onet, Manet, Rubens, Van Dyck. These were names I had heard since infancy. These had been masters of their art, their medium being the one my mother most wanted to master herself and the one that she worked hardest to perfect.

Watercolors.

This I knew about watercolors. They are delicate and vulnerable to the elements. They can be intense or subtle, depending on what they are mixed with. They can be transparent, letting what is underneath shine through to add its own color to the paint, that being left to the discretion of the artist.

And they are unforgiving. Watercolors stain as soon as they touch the paper and therefore cannot be undone as can oils on canvas. The skilled artist, though, can use the mistake to his or her advantage, painting around it with other hues, incorporating it into the picture. Mistakes can be disastrous or ingenious, depending heavily on the eye and heart of the artist.

'm more concerned about Kat than I am about myself."
It was one of many late-night back-porch conversations that I eaves-
dropped upon between my mother and Jeanette. Most every night
after dinner had been served and the dishes put away, the two would sit
in rocking chairs, drink coffee, and talk. Their rocking and sometimes
their conversation would end up in sync with not only each other, but
with the quiet gulf roar as well. At low tide, the breakers on the shore
were diminished to rhythmic, demure purrs. The seagulls and beach-
combers were in for the night, and so the quietest moments were late in
the evening. It was at this time that I could overhear what my mother was
thinking. And it was at this time that I could vacillate between despair
and serenity so quickly. The pulse of the sounds could swing me from
one extreme to the other in seconds.

I waited for Jeanette's response to my mother's concern for me.
Finally Jeanette rocked forward and turned slowly.

"Chan, this ain't right, your separatin'. It ain't right. I know I haven't
said nuthin' 'cause I didn't think it was my bidness. You know me, I don't
like to pry in other folk's affairs, but it ain't never right to break the holy
bonds of matrimony."

For once, I wanted to hug Jeanette.

"Oh, Jeanette. You don't understand. George and I have just drifted
apart."

"So, just drift back together, you two. If for no other reason, but for
that little girl in there."

Hurray for the sentiment, but I took offense at the reference to my
being a little girl.

"That's why George and I have stayed together this long. For Kat's sake. But there comes a point at which it's not good for her to see her parents stay in a loveless marriage either."

"Ah..." Jeanette was about to balk.

"I know," Mama continued. "Love is a choice and so if we'd just choose—"

"Love is a gift, missy. A gift from God Almighty!" I hadn't heard Jeanette ever use such an aggressive tone with my mother.

I couldn't see it, but I could imagine my mother's face was a mixture of surprise with an added smirk of condescension. I had heard Jeanette tell my mother that she had never been married, but that she had had a suitor who had been killed in World War II, so I was anticipating the next bit of conversation.

Jeanette continued, "I know what you're thinkin', Chan. You're thinking, 'What does that old maid know about love?'" She did not pause for a response. "Well, I can tell you straight up that God never smiles on divorce, and that's right out of the Good Book."

"Oh?"

My mother was an agnostic. She had informed me of that fact every time I had attended church with my father and grandparents. They were Methodists. "Casual Methodists," I heard someone say once. I didn't understand the comment, but I understood the inference. I took it to mean that the Mortons were so labeled because they did not regularly attend services at First Church. I noted, however, that they were members in high regard because of their generous contributions to the offering plate and were usually greeted warmly by the pastor and other members.

"Only mindless hicks would buy into religion," my mother had said once when I asked her something about God. I had been surprised at her candor, for it implied that I was a mindless hick if I believed. I think her comment was not directed to me but at that moment was more an unearthing of her apparent loathing of her in-laws' religious affiliation and, I guessed, my father's. She never made that comment again, probably because I never asked her anything about God again.

Chapter Fourteen

H ey, Barry." I had finally gotten up the nerve to return to the Hang-out in the new swimsuit and orange-tinted hair. It had taken a week of sunning to even out the tan, which was still not even, but I was close enough.

"Hey." The bronzed lifeguard glanced at me as he passed by. I had been sitting on the bench on the edge of the dance floor for half an hour watching the beach, where he had been sitting under an umbrella in a faded fabric chair emblazoned with Ed's Beach Service in large white letters. I figured that the two lifeguards on duty would rotate so that they could each take bathroom and food breaks. I didn't know the rotation schedule, but I was prepared to stay there until Barry walked by. And that's all Barry did finally was walk by and lamely return my greeting. However, I knew he'd have to return to the beach sooner or later, and I'd have a chance to speak to him again and hopefully catch his eye. I could wait. I had all day. Jeanette and Mama had both been glued to the TV set for days after the launch of the Apollo 11 mission that was supposed to put the first man on the moon. I was not interested myself in anything past the gravitational pull of my own planet, but I was glad that the subtle changes I was making and my longer-than-usual walks on the beach would largely go unnoticed.

"Kath-a-leen?"

Oh, no. It was Malcolm for sure. I didn't even need to turn around. Apparently he had followed me.

"What in the world are you doing here, Malcolm?" I said without looking over my shoulder. He was probably standing there wearing his Hawaiian flowered shorts and his favorite shirt, the one with his name printed on the front. Trying not to look like I was regarding him in any way, I kept my back to him while watching for Barry to return.

"What are you doing here, Kath-a-leen?"

"Hanging out, Malcolm. It's called the Hangout. That's what people do here. They hang out."

Malcolm guffawed, punctuating his laughter with Popeye yucks.

"That's funny, Kath-a-leen."

"Yes, it is. Now please leave."

It was Saturday afternoon and the beaches were full of sunbathers. The open-air dance hall was dotted with teenagers sitting on the benches around the perimeter of the dance floor. There was a steady stream of songs being played on the jukebox, all of which I knew and could sing along to. It made me feel older and, I was assuming, made me look more mature that I was an aficionado of the top forty.

"Wanna dance?"

I wheeled around to chide Malcolm for even asking but saw a boy about my age looking awkward and sunburned. "Sure."

I scanned the floor for Barry, and then I looked around for Malcolm. Neither was in sight.

The headline read, "The Eagle Has Landed." The newspaper lay on the kitchen table next to the doughnuts and orange juice Jeanette had left for us. It was Sunday morning and I knew that she and Malcolm had gone to church. Sunday was the only day that Jeanette didn't cook a full break-fast. She did, however, serve a hot meal—usually fried chicken, mashed potatoes, and field peas—around one o'clock in the afternoon. It was my favorite food day since I hated bacon and eggs but loved chicken and mashed potatoes.

"I'm gonna be a astronaut," Malcolm announced before stuffing a forkful of potatoes in his mouth.

"You are?" Jeanette mused. The dinner table had only us four around it. The other two artists who were staying there for the summer had gone to paint other places near the beach. One quiet but creepy woman named

Maureen had said she was going to paint near the jetties. Most of the paintings I'd seen of hers were not very good, not as good as Mama's at least. Maureen worked with oils and seemed to be a beginner, yet she was persistent and was gone a lot.

The other artist at the colony was a man named Guy who seemed to have a nice touch on the canvas. At least that's what Mama said about him. Guy was, I guessed, ten years older than my father, but not as refined. Guy loved to tell semi-crude jokes and drink lots of beer. I could tell that he was attracted to my mother by the way he eyed her from a distance. But then again, who wasn't attracted to my mother? Apparently my father was the only one.

Chapter Fifteen

"Hey, Kat, what do you say we go to Miracle Strip tonight?" Mama asked one late July afternoon.

"I'd rather go to the Hangout." I answered before I really thought about it. Up until that point I hadn't talked to my mother about the teen dance hall I'd discovered and frequented. It seemed in those days that neither Mama, nor anyone else for that matter, had noticed or cared where I went or what I did with my time. No one except Malcolm, who often was just ten steps behind me.

"Hangout? Where's that?"

"Uh, it's down at Long Beach."

"Oh, you mean that open-air dance hall thing?"

"Yeah." I hoped the conversation would cease at that point. Even though I was fairly sure the Hangout wasn't an evil place for a thirteen-year-old girl, it was my place. There I could be among teenagers I didn't know and therefore imagine myself to be exciting or mysterious or anonymous if I chose. I could dance with a stranger or sit and watch the others. I could sing along to the music and laugh at the way the rhythm of the sand underneath sandaled feet was most of the time out of rhythm with the song. It was my place and I could be whoever I wanted to be there.

"Well, if you don't want to go to Miracle Strip with us, that's fine." Mama was sitting in a chair by the window with a sketchpad and a pencil, hard at work sketching a scene she had eyed down the beach. That was the thing I hated most about her. She was forever focused on a sight somewhere out past me, out past us, out past reality, and when she did regard me, I felt it to be an aside.

"Us?" Though I had hoped not to continue the conversation, but the shock of that word was too hard to hide.

Mama finally looked up from her sketch, and my eyes and hers met for the first time in I couldn't remember when.

"Yeah, I thought you, me, Guy, maybe Malcolm might go over and ride the Starliner a few times."

Malcolm wouldn't ride the roller coaster. He had watched Mama and me ride it a few times and had gotten nauseated just sitting on a bench nearby.

"I don't like the noise," he would say, putting his hands over his ears. I had thought perhaps the rattle of the coaster cars over the wooden frame and the squeal of the brakes as it stopped were too shrill for his ears. But I soon realized that the screams of the riders were what bothered him the most. I'd thought it silly at first, but knowing a bit about his history as I did, I wondered if he had memories of his parents and if those memories included screaming.

"Guy?" I cocked my head at my mother. It was as if she had been waiting for this moment to speak her colleague's name to me in a casual way and to capture my response.

"Yeah. He asked this morning if we wanted to go. I told him I'd have to ask you."

What I remember most about that moment was that all things started to make sense. I was almost thankful for the clarity, I'm sure, but the revelation itself sent me out the door and into a full jog down the beach.

I felt both ridiculous and serene propped up on a post under the pier. I couldn't control the tears, but I was most concerned that my audible sobs would draw someone's attention. A wave broke close to my feet, and I watched the periwinkles that the surf coughed up bury themselves in the soft sand. At that moment, I wanted to be one of the periwinkles. I wanted to bury myself forever.

I had never really gotten the lyrics of the song when I listened to it on the radio, but when I heard it played on the jukebox that night, I caught every word and it called out to me. The Fifth Dimension may have called "Aquarius" just another hit song, but for me it was a cosmic message. Though I had no idea what the alignment of planets had to do with me and my life, I was determined to find out.

"I dig this song, don't you?"

Barry looked up at me from the bench and slowly pulled his shades down on his nose.

"'Scuse me?"

"This song. 'Aquarius,'" I said before realizing that three more songs had played on the jukebox since "Aquarius." It had taken me that long to get up the nerve to approach Barry, and so I hadn't truly noticed what was playing at that moment. I tried to cover. "Well, I know this isn't..."

"It's aw-ight." It was the first time I had heard Barry speak except for the first time when he tried to introduce himself to me. I hadn't noticed the Southern good-ol'-boy drawl before. I tried to decide if this was endearing. I hoped it would be. However, he wasn't appearing as I had dreamed: sophisticated, yet still boyish; intelligent, yet slow to let it show.

"It's hard to dance to. I like 'Unchained Melodies' myself."

I tried to overlook the fact that the hit song was actually called "Unchained Melody," because I certainly didn't want to correct him. "Oh, yes, I love the Righteous Brothers, too. 'You've Lost That Lovin' Feelin,' 'Soul and Inspiration.' I've got their LPs at home and the 45s here with me."

Barry smiled and pushed the shades back up on his nose and returned his gaze to the surf. "How old are you?"

"Uh, old enough to know better." I didn't know where I'd heard that meaningless retort, but I hoped it would put him off so I could keep my true age a secret.

"No, really. How old are you? Fourteen?"

"Good guess, but I'll be fifteen in August. Be getting my permit soon."

"Huh." He didn't sound as though he believed me. "Where you from?"

At least he was willing to continue the conversation.

"Uh, here. PC." I shortened *Panama City* the way the locals did. "Well, it's our summer home. We winter in Baltimore." I was thinking fast, pulling out half-truths that could have led anywhere.

"Oh."

Before I could read his response, a whistle blew above us. Barry jumped to his feet and yelled to the boy up on the lifeguard tower. "Hey Greg, what da see up 'ere?"

Until now they'd rotated every hour or so from tower to beach umbrella. Not a care in the world. But now Greg and Barry were sprinting toward the gulf, Greg carrying a life preserver tied to a long rope that was wound loosely and slung over his shoulder.

The whole scene was like an old silent movie, a series of individual frames that don't move fast enough to make it look real. A woman stood on the beach, pointing to the surf. Her eyes showed panic and she was screaming unintelligibly. With fluid movements, the two boys took their positions. Barry stood near the water like an anchor holding the circle of rope while Greg splashed into the water and then swam with determination to a small dot that had just come into my view. It seemed to be a blur of red plastic float, flailing arms, and blond hair. I couldn't tell if it was a boy or a girl in trouble, but it was obviously the child of the woman on the beach. Barry let out the rope as quickly as Greg swam, and when the rope looked as though it was at its end, Barry followed it into the surf. Within seconds, it seemed, Greg was swimming back toward us with the child in tow. Barry was winding the rope again in the loose circle around his shoulder. By that time, most of the people who had been sitting on the beach were gathered at the scene, one woman wrapping her arms around the frightened mother.

"I'm a doctor," a man shouted, running down the beach. Though the jukebox was still playing on, most of the dancers had emptied out onto the sand.

Greg started walking when the water was about knee deep, keeping the face of the child, who looked limp and lifeless, above the water. The moment he hit level beach, the mother, the doctor, and two other people rushed to grab the child, who immediately sprang to life and started crying. Applause arose on the beach. While the doctor and the lifeguards attended to the child, who by this time I could tell was a boy, I watched the red plastic float bob in the water a few times. I returned my attention to the rescue scene for a few seconds, but when I looked back out to find the float, it had disappeared.

Chapter Sixteen

I felt drained. My anger at Mama's hints that she was dating Guy hadn't yet subsided when the drama of the water rescue stole what energy I had left. I sat, sulking on the sand, trying to decide how to react to my parents' disregard for my feelings. Self-pity consumed me. I tried to think through my options. Go back to the cabin and protest? Find a way home to try and reason with my father? Or simply run away from it all?

I had no money. I had run out of the cabin so abruptly that any preparation I could have made to run away was forgotten, and so I sat back under the pier as the sun set over the gulf. No one would miss me until, perhaps, bedtime. Would they get worried and come looking for me? I figured Malcolm at least wondered where I was and maybe Jeanette did, too. But as far as I knew, Mama and Guy were laughing together as they boarded the Starliner at Miracle Strip Amusement Park.

Three seagulls came in to land on the beach, and they waddled toward me to see if I had any food for them. Gulls had enough experience with tourists to know they could swindle a few of them out of breadcrumbs or popcorn. I had nothing to give them. I couldn't even feed myself at that moment, but I was determined not to return to the cabin or home to Jackson. Not then, maybe not ever.

"Kat?"

The voice I heard didn't sound like Malcolm, and yet I turned, expecting to see him there. "Malcolm?" I brightened, kind of hoping to see his funny face.

It wasn't Malcolm. It was my mother, standing at a distance with her arms folded. I couldn't speak. Her arms reached toward me. Somehow I got to my feet and met her embrace.

The water suddenly leaped up to my waist, taking my breath away, and I jumped up, trying to get out of its way. It was then that I realized I had dozed off. I looked down at my soaking shorts and then behind me. What part of the last scene had happened and what part had I dreamed?

"Mama?"

All I could see was mostly deserted beach. Even the lifeguards had packed up their equipment and left for the day. The dance hall was starting to fill with the teenaged night crowd. I was wet and sticky and sandy and hungry. And alone.

The waves sparkled as they broke on the sand. I had asked Mama once what made the gulf water look like glitter at night. She had said something about phosphorus in the water, but the way she described the sight of it stuck with me more than its cause. She said it looked like diamonds on lace. And that was what lifted my spirits while I walked aimlessly down the beach.

I heard the music before I saw the fire. The sounds of guitars were accompanied by voices barely audible over the strumming. A few steps more and I could see the orange glow of a fire rising on the other side of the next dune. A campfire sing-along. It was a typical sight on the beach. I thought this might be a scout group or a band of hippies, and so I hesitated a second or two before I decided to approach.

"Jesus, Jesus. Jesus in the morning, Jesus in the noontime. Jesus, Jesus. Jesus when the sun goes down."

Definitely not a scout group, but Jesus freak hippies were a possibility.

It was then the smell hit me and I remembered how hungry I was. Hot dogs on an open fire. Like a ravenous dog I quickened my stride into a full jog.

"Hey." The music stopped. I remember the group looking a little startled when I spoke, but then I realized that my presence was not perhaps the big surprise, but it had been my tone and volume. I must have looked and sounded a little desperate.

"Hey," a boy, or maybe a man, holding a guitar answered. He rose from the beach towel he had been sitting on, handed his guitar to a girl, or maybe a woman, sitting next to him. Neither of them looked like hippies to me, but then again I didn't have a good grasp on how to identify a true hippie.

"Join us?" the man asked me. Heads nodded, and a girl rose from a piece of driftwood she and a few others were using as a bench. The girl walked toward me, and I could see as she approached that she was probably the age of a college student.

"We've got hot dogs and cokes." She took my arm and led me toward the fire.

At that point, my survival-by-pretense instinct kicked in. "I'd rather have a beer, if you've got it."

A few giggles rose from the group. The girl smiled. "All we've got are Cokes and Tab. We've also got some marshmallows."

The faces of the others around the fire became a blur as I focused on the hot dog the girl handed me.

Restraint passed through my mind, and it kept me from shoving the whole hot dog into my mouth, and I quickly realized that all eyes of the twenty or so people around the campfire were glued on me. I stopped my second bite in midstream and remembered my manners.

"Thank you, this is very good," I managed to say, hiding my first bite in my cheek.

"You're welcome. We were just having a little sing-along." The man with the guitar reached into a cooler and pulled out a bottle of Coke. He produced a bottle opener from his shirt pocket, popped open the drink and handed it to me. I grabbed the cold bottle with my free hand.

"Good," I said, motioning with the bottle a gesture that meant, "Please proceed. Don't let me bother you." Then I noticed for the first time that everyone was staring at me. They were all basically the same age, older than I, maybe late teens. It occurred to me, too, that some of the faces I might find to be familiar, those I'd seen at the Hangout from time to time, but there was no one I recognized. Slowly, their gaze drifted from me back to the fire, for which I was glad. I finished the hot dog in four more bites.

The guitar player retrieved his guitar and returned to his spot on the sand. He began to strum randomly.

"You live around here?" someone to my right asked. I turned to find a pretty blond girl holding a straightened coat hanger with two marsh-mallows dangling from the end. It took me a couple of seconds to realize she was talking to me.

"Oh, yeah. I live here…some of the time." I was trying to remember the wording of the lie I had told Lifeguard Barry. All I could remember was something about summering here and wintering in Baltimore. I decided to try that.

"Baltimore?" came a voice from the driftwood bench. "I'm from Baltimore. What part?"

I took a deep breath and tried to recall anything I had heard my mother say about her roots.

"South." That would buy me some time, I hoped, before the girl asked me another question.

"Oh, South Baltimore. Well, I'm from Hampden, north of the city," she answered. I tried to detect whether her tone of voice when she said "South Baltimore" was the least bit condescending as if it were a seedy part of town. But more than that, I hoped the girl would drop the inter-rogation altogether because I couldn't for the life of me think of anything about the city that would actually put my residence there. Fortunately the man with the guitar launched into another song and the others joined in. I eyed the several coat hangers with marshmallows on them being roasted at that moment and tried not to salivate. Just then a person to my left handed me my own coat hanger with three marshmallows, which I immediately thrust into the open fire.

"What's your name?" the guy who gave me the marshmallows asked.

"My name?" I tried to decide whether to tell him the truth.

"Yeah, my name's Paul."

"Oh, well, I'm…Kathleen." What harm could it do to say my real name? It would save confusion later on if I had one less lie to remember.

"Nice to meet you, Kathleen. Were we making too much noise or something with our singing?"

"Huh?"

"You sounded annoyed when you first walked up. Thought maybe we were being too loud and you could hear us from your house."

I shook my head.

For the first time, I actually looked into the eyes of one of the people seated around the fire. Paul seemed to be the same age as the others. I couldn't tell how tall he was because he was seated like me. I could tell that he was clean cut and shaven, not like the hippies I'd heard about, so I wondered what drew these people together at this place and moment in time.

"I'm a Taurus," I said, just trying to make conversation.

Paul looked at me with a little bit of surprise. "Oh?"

"Yeah, that means I'm patient and reliable." I had read about horoscopes in *Fave Magazine* right after I heard the song "Aquarius." The article had also described my kind as jealous and possessive, resentful and inflexible, self-indulgent and greedy, but I chose not to reveal those qualities.

"Really? That's nice. I'm sure you are." I detected that Paul was uncomfortable with my statement for some reason, and he turned his attention back to the group singing.

"I've got peace like a river, I've got peace like a river, I've got peace like a river in my soul."

It was a simple melody with, frankly, overly simplistic words, but for some reason I didn't understand at all what it meant. I reasoned, however, that I hadn't understood "Row, Row, Row Your Boat" either but had decided that it was a nonsense song that was just fun to sing. After the first chorus of "Peace Like a River," I sang along, finding out to my embarrassment that the word *peace* was changed to *love* and *joy* for the following verses. No one seemed to notice my error because they were all involved in singing and clapping to the music. A man stood up, smiled, and started to talk in a pleasant voice.

By the time the man had finished talking, the fire had died down. He had read from a small Bible, not like the cumbersome one that sat on the large table at the front of the Methodist church back home. And when the man had said words like *thee* and *thou* and regular words that ended in *eth*, they didn't sound awkward as they had as when Reverend Harper had spoken them. I was a little amazed, too, at the attention that the group gave to this man. I had noticed while he was speaking that he was not a boy or even a teenager like many of the others. He was older, a man, maybe the age of my father. And when I realized that fact, my heart began to ache.

My clothes had dried and my stomach was full, but I was really tired as if I hadn't slept in a couple of days. I reviewed the past several hours in my mind and realized that it wasn't a lack of sleep, nor the late hour, that had exhausted me so. It was the fact that I had not so many hours behind me in my journey, but many more to come.

I said good-bye to Paul and the others who had said it to me and I kept going down the beach. I had no thoughts of where I might go, I just followed the shoreline. But somewhat unexpectedly, it turned, and then ended at a large building with a dock jutting out from it. As I moved closer I could see some fishing boats bobbing next to the dock. They were all dark inside, and I wondered how far any one of them might take me away from my life.

Chapter Seventeen

I must have been more exhausted than I had imagined. I awoke from what was a deep sleep with no idea how long I had been there. It was morning. I could tell that even through the tarp I had wrapped myself in to camouflage my presence on the deck of one of the boats. I grabbed an edge of the tarp and drew it closer to me, hoping that I could stay hidden from the owner of the boat I had commandeered. I wondered if my mother had called the police. Had she called my father? Had she even noticed that I was gone?

"Hot coffee," I heard a woman shout nearby. I couldn't tell whether she was on the next boat or standing in the galley of mine.

Slowly I pushed the tarp off my face enough to peek one eye to check. I was relieved to discover that the woman and a man were just boarding a boat two slips down. The man was untying the boat as the woman was carrying on a large picnic basket. It was then I recognized hunger again.

A motor grinded and a propeller sputtered and the boat backed out of the slip, taking the man and woman away.

A quick glance around the dock let me know there weren't any other people around that I could see. So I thought I should make a quick exit before anyone appeared, but I also didn't want to make a run for it without knowing where I was running. The building I had seen the night before, I discovered, was a restaurant. The sign said Captain Anderson's. I hoped this restaurant hadn't opened yet for the day, and that I could sneak around and find some food. Uncovering myself, I stepped off the boat and said a silent thank-you to the owner for letting it give me temporary shelter.

No luck. The restaurant was abandoned, for which I was grateful, but not even a morsel of food was at my disposal. The garbage cans behind the kitchen had been emptied. I thought of the night before at the campfire and wished I had asked for one more hot dog.

"Hey, Baltimore." I hadn't wanted to backtrack. I had wanted to move on, but I returned to where I thought the campsite might have been to look for leftover food. I hadn't found any, but the girl from Baltimore I'd had a brief conversation with the night before had returned to bury the ashes the group had left behind.

My instinct made me turn away from the voice, but I thought quickly enough to stop and face her. I didn't want to give away the fact that I was a runaway.

"Hey." She waved. I waved back. As she walked toward me, I tried hard to remember what I'd told her the night before. "Kathleen, is it?"

"Yeah, how did you know?"

"Paul said at our evening prayer time that he'd talked to you a little and that you'd told him your name."

"Yeah, Paul's a cool guy." I realized I was wearing the same clothes I had worn at the campfire, but hoped Baltimore wouldn't notice.

"You're out early." The girl picked up a shovel and started pouring sand on the charred wood.

"Yeah, I like to get up early. It's quiet and I can think."

"Me too." She didn't look up from her task. "I usually do my quiet time from six to seven o'clock at school. My roommate likes to sleep later when she doesn't have an early class, and really nobody's up much in the dorm. I don't know about you, but I can't concentrate on the Lord like I should when there's a lot going on around me."

"Yeah, me neither. Well, I've gotta get going. I haven't even said my morning prayers yet." If nothing else, I had learned to fit in, to speak the language everyone else was speaking. It seemed easier that way, though a few times it had backfired on me.

"Hey, we're having a game night tonight up at the cabin. You're welcome to join us."

"Oh, I'm not…"

"It's okay. It's real informal. The Bible study part of this retreat is mostly during the day, and at night we just hang out and fellowship."

"Hang out?" I was hoping I could mention my experience at the dance hall and appear more sophisticated. "You been there much?"

"What?"

"The Hangout, down at Long Beach."

"Oh, no. We just got here last night. The bonfire was kind of our first thing of the retreat."

"Oh." I hadn't ever heard of a retreat, but since this girl and the others I had seen the night before were apparently in college, I figured the event would be something I could experience one day when I got to college. That is, if I ever made it that far.

"Well, bye." I said, not remembering if I had told anyone which direction my home was in.

"Bye." The girl looked up with a smile and a small smudge of ash on her face. She went back to her task, and I walked toward the cottages that lined the beach. It must have been rather early still because there were few people stirring. I had to admit, I liked the quiet times, too, but I'd never wanted to get up early to find them.

Clothes flapped in the morning wind behind me outside a cottage. Hanging clothes outside was a common sight around beach houses and hotels. Jeanette hung our swimsuits and towels on the clothesline at the colony, hoping to keep them from souring. She had said, however, that with the humidity like it was in midsummer, "It don't do no good." But the clothes hanging before me gave me an idea.

As I sat on a dune and looked at the morning surf, I thought not only about Jeanette, but also about Mama and Daddy, and Malcolm. At that moment, they were my world, and when I had convinced myself that they didn't care where I was I started to cry. Salt tears stung my face and ran into my mouth. I was slightly distracted from my self-pity by wondering if my tears had phosphorus in them like gulf water and would sparkle at night. It was a silly thought, but I was satisfied that it was at least poetic. Somewhere out of my thoughts, I pulled "Peace Like A River." The tune was still there and, of course, the simple words. But as I started to sing it, I realized I didn't have peace. If anything I had the opposite. What was the opposite of peace? War? Anger? Rage? I felt inside like there was a churning of the surf at high tide. I changed the words to "I've got rage like an ocean," wiped the tears, and found a resolve to keep running.

The beach didn't just end, it turned inland. I had followed it the night before where I had found Captain Anderson's, the dock, and the boat that would be my bed for the night. I was curious, however, to see where the road continued to. Maybe it meandered and would put me back on the sandy beach eventually. I walked past the restaurant and saw that the road didn't meander at all, but spilled onto a major highway. At the intersection, I could tell this wasn't just a crossroad, but a dead end for me. To the right was a bridge that spanned farther than I could see. To the left were shops and hotels and short-order food places. I didn't feel safe taking either turn. On the outside chance that my mother had indeed missed me and had called the police, I didn't want to risk letting someone see me on a main thoroughfare. I would have to stay on the beach. It was the only place where I could maintain anonymity long enough to figure out what to do next. I did know, however, that I would not go back to the artist colony. There was nothing for me there. I had to decide whether to try for home. And then a familiar fear hit me. What if there was nothing there for me either?

Chapter Eighteen

The cotton shorts were a little loose, but at least they were fashionable. I silently thanked the girl or woman who had "donated" them to me, as worthy a cause as I could imagine. I had to go to three more clotheslines to find a shirt that was plain, not too colorful and without a recognizable logo. Because I wasn't sure where to go, I decided to blend into the beach environment for a while and pander for survival. I would have to be careful. I couldn't raise suspicion nor stay in one place for long. I had heard someone say that these beaches stretched some twenty miles, so I figured I could hide by blending in and dodging crowded, public places. I would stay away from the exposure of the shoreline, too. There were enough beach houses and small hotels that would protect me from any search that may have been launched for me. I was struck again with the notion that maybe no one was even looking for me.

I headed toward a tiny pond created by the backwaters of the last evening's high tide. The water was tepid and went up to my mid-calf, but it was refreshing and soothing to my feet that were scorched by the hot sand. I watched the surf roll toward my pond, trying to recapture it and sweep it back out again. But the body of water was stubbornly holding its ground, refusing to let itself go back to its origin. I was proud of myself for seeing this as an analogy, for thinking deep enough thoughts to take this as a sign that I should hold my ground, too. I would refuse to be swept back in again to the churning tide of my family's selfish struggles. They didn't need me. I didn't need them.

The sun was quickly moving to midday, and more hunger was moving in, too. The smell of bacon cooking was coming from a nearby beach house. I thought of all the bacon Jeanette had fried for me that I had refused. At that moment I regretted those refusals. The smell was strong but I didn't dare follow it. Instead I moved in the opposite direction, feeling that somehow the aroma was a lure that would hook me too soon. I thought about the "retreat" people I had met and made a mental note that this could be a haven should I need it. Those people had seemed kind and trustworthy, and I would expect them to help me should I ask for it.

Plunging my hands into my newfound shorts, I was almost too surprised to believe what I felt. Could it be? I pulled a faded five-dollar bill out of the pocket, then instinctively ran toward the nearest dune for cover. It was a miracle! I had never experienced a miracle before and had not even been sure that they existed.

I thought of…what was her name? Baltimore. Had she told me her name? And what was the guy's name? Paul, maybe. Baltimore had said they had prayed for me. Maybe this was what they had prayed, that I would find money in my pocket. No, I had stolen the shorts. I didn't know much about God, but I did know He frowned upon stealing. There had to be another force guiding me, providing for me. I was sure the planets were aligning in my favor. I looked to the sky and shaded my eyes from the scorching sun. I wondered if the astronauts were still bouncing around on the moon, and then I was worried that somehow they would cause a disturbance in whatever cosmic force that was in play. I clasped the five-dollar bill between my hands and scrubbed them back and forth as though the bill were a genie's lamp. I made a wish and headed down the beach to find the nearest food stand.

Chapter Nineteen

I was proud of myself. I had made five dollars go a long way. I figured that by drinking water from beach house spigots, I could feed and water myself almost a week. It had already been two days since I found the money in the pocket of my stolen shorts, and I had almost three dollars left. Sleeping on beach chairs left out to dry by tourists hadn't been the most desirable bedding, but it was adequate, especially with the addition of a borrowed beach towel. There was no shortage of shower facilities either. Most of the houses and motels had showers outside and in the evenings I could use them to "freshen" a bit. Even clothing was abundant. So far, however, I had not found another pocket full of money, but the cosmos would provide. I was sure of that.

The third day of freedom. The night before I had rested peacefully in the fact that I was making it on my own, but when the sun rose that morning, I had a different feeling. I still had the resources to survive a few more days, but for some reason I felt bound again. Even the twenty-mile stretch of beach seemed too small for me. Oh, I could stay hidden for a while in the powder-white world of Northwest Florida, I was sure, but I groaned inside to think that this would forever be my world. That seemed more restraining and isolating than the world I had left behind. So, what should I wish for? A one-dollar bill probably wouldn't bring me as much fortune as a five would, but I rubbed it anyway and wished for a sign of what was to be my next move.

The voices did not seem casual, as lovers on the beach might sound. These were whispers of a more serious nature, almost like the conversations my mother and Jeanette had had on the porch at night. The thought of them suddenly caused a churning in my stomach that I tried to ignore.

The moon was half full, but it didn't give enough light for me to see very far down the beach. Most of the renters had turned off their lights for the evening, so when I opened my eyes I could not see the people talking, though they sounded nearby.

I shifted in my beach chair to make enough noise for someone to realize I was there, but not enough to startle them.

The voices stopped suddenly. It concerned me and I sat still again. Maybe they had passed me by or perhaps they had been lovers after all and were retreating toward another dune for some privacy.

I listened. I waited.

The sudden light made me react with a quick move of the beach towel to cover my face. What? Can't you see I'm sleeping here?

"Miss?" A male voice seemed to come from the light source.

I froze.

A hand peeled back the covering on my face, and the center of the light hit me again. This was definitely an authority figure, probably a policeman on beach patrol. It was the first time I had encountered such an authority.

"Miss? Do you have some identification?" he asked again.

"Yes." What was I saying? I had no identification. "No. Not with me." Survive.

I pointed to the nearest structure. "I'm from Baltimore, staying in that house, and my parents said it was all right if I slept out here. I didn't know it was wrong."

"That's her." A softer voice, not the patrolman's.

Trying to shield my eyes from the invasive light, I recognized the voice. Paul, the man from the campfire.

"What? No, I told you—" But before I could manufacture another defense, the large hand clasped around my arm and I was being prodded gently from my chair. I chose not to resist because I was still planning to maintain my innocence or launch an escape.

"I'm sorry, Kathleen," Paul said. "We were afraid for you. You need to be home with your family." The policeman started to lead me away.

What had happened? How had they known I was there? Who had cared I was gone?

The policeman with the large hands wrapped the beach towel around my shoulders, and when he did, the blinding light drifted to the others with him. Yes, it was Paul…and Baltimore girl. My heart sank. My cosmic luck had run out. The retreat people had turned me in. How had they known I was a runaway? How could they have betrayed me? How could I escape?

Chapter Twenty

Were so worried about you, honey." My father's voice sounded shaky and tired.

I didn't look up. I didn't want to even try to take it all in. My father, my mother, and my grandmother Morton were all standing in a line with their arms folded in front of them. In the background were Jeanette, Malcolm, Guy, Maureen, and the man whose hand had ensnared me on the beach. Apparently, Paul and the Baltimore girl were too ashamed of their betrayal to attend this late-night tribunal.

"What are you doing here?" I was surprised at the vile tone that came out of my mouth.

Mimi spoke first and sat beside me. "Why, we were worried sick about you, dear, and your grandfather called every lawman in Bay County to look for you." She looked up and said for their benefit, "Everett knows the sheriff down here." I wasn't affected by the honey dripping in her voice anymore as I once had been. This time I made note of the content. By my grandmother's own admission my grandfather had not seen fit to come himself to look for me, but that he called his "people" to do his work. I was surprised that she had come. It must have been hard for her to break away from her garden club duties to look for her missing raven-haired granddaughter.

"I wasn't talking to you." Finally, I looked up into my father's eyes. It was then that I noticed Malcolm in the distance, leaning against the wall, crying. I could see his mouth moving. "Oh boy," he kept repeating.

My father crouched before me and tried to look at me. I turned away. My mother hadn't said a word. She wasn't crying either.

Daddy sat down on the other side of me. "Kat, honey. We are so blessed that we found you safe and sound. Why, these past few days…"

"Blessed," Jeanette said. "Yeah. Sug-ah, we stayed up and kept a prayer vigil goin' for you. The Lord delivered you to our hands. I just know it. Praise the Lord!" And when her hands went up, her tears started to fall.

"Bee-bee…" Daddy's soft, sincere words almost melted me. When I looked at his weary, unshaven face, I could see his concern and relief. But I held my ground, vowing silently to never let him in again. He drew me to him in his strong arms and I relaxed a bit, secretly welcoming the embrace.

Still my mother said nothing. Her stance told me all I needed to know. She was angry with me. I ventured a guess that she was angry because I had interrupted her creative flow, or her plans with Guy, or angry that I had brought my father and grandmother to witness her obvious lack of care for me.

Well, I was angry, too. Raging. Ready to run again.

I can hear you, you know, I thought. Apparently I had fallen asleep on the couch before my accusers, but that hadn't stopped them from talking about my plight. I kept my eyes closed.

"She needs help."

"She needs a spanking."

"It's all my fault."

Trying to apply sentiments to voices, I surmised that Jeanette was sympathetic, my mother was still angry, and my father felt guilty.

"She needs a doctor." My grandmother was still in the room. I heard nothing from Malcolm or the others.

I wasn't really comfortable dressed in someone else's clothes, wrapped in someone else's soured beach towel, and lying on a hard leather couch, but I was determined to stay there faking sleep until they all left me alone. I don't know when real sleep happened, but when I opened my eyes, it was daylight and I was alone.

The sound of someone shuffling around in the kitchen made me think Jeanette was starting early breakfast preparations. I would start to smell the sausage patties frying soon. I had most of the time turned up my nose at Jeanette's country breakfasts, opting for dry toast or cereal, but at that moment, sausage and eggs were what I craved the most. That and vengeance.

With one eye, I carefully looked around the room. I saw no one. Figuring this to be a good time to make a quick trip to the bathroom, I swung my legs off the couch thinking they would soon meet up with the floor. Instead, they landed on the soft belly of a person.

"Malcolm!" He looked as startled as I, but I was more concerned about my announcing my waking than I was about whether I had hurt him. Malcolm rolled away from the couch and up onto his knees. Then I could see that he had been lying on a palette of the blanket and pillow from his bed. He stood up and blinked at me past swollen eyes and disheveled hair.

"Kath-a-leen, you're awake."

"Shhhh. Go back to sleep, Malcolm," I said, hoping he would obey. He just stood and looked at me with a mixture of wonder and pain in his eyes.

"I'm just going to the restroom," I said, and he stepped out of the way to let me pass.

The room I had shared with my mother was empty. Our beds looked like they had not been slept in. I could only imagine where my mother was sleeping now. Then I realized she wasn't sleeping at all, but standing right behind me. I turned to see that she still had the stern look she had had the night before. She did not speak, but raised an eyebrow as if to say, "Well, where are you going?"

Before she asked, I mumbled something about needing to use the bathroom.

The image in the bathroom mirror frightened me. My hair was greasy and matted from days of not washing it with shampoo. My face looked bonier than usual and the clothes I had on, even I didn't recognize. But I peeled them off and welcomed a long, soothing shower. Knowing that my mother was probably standing on the other side of the door, I took my time. I didn't just dread seeing her, or talking to her, I was pretty sure I loathed her.

Chapter Twenty-one

M y parents sat on the old leather couch, looking like a mismatched pair of shoes. Unbalanced. Uncomfortable. Opposites of each other. My mother sat as she usually did, on the edge of the seat with her legs crossed and then crossed again, twisted like a pretzel. My father sat forward, too with his elbows on his knees, hands clasped in front of him. Their body language told me immediately that they were at odds about something, probably my fate, and that I had interrupted a spirited discussion they had been having about me.

Daddy managed a weak smile. Mama looked away. My grandmother was nowhere to be found. I assumed she'd had her driver take her back to Jackson now that the wayward child had been found. I didn't care. I didn't care. I didn't care.

"How do you feel?" Daddy asked me as I stood in front of a wall mirror in the living room and tried to brush the kinks out of my wet hair.

I shrugged.

"So, you're okay?"

"Yeah." That's all I had planned to surrender, but I just had to add, "Who wants to know?"

"Don't talk to your father that way, young lady." They were the first words my mother had spoken to me in several days.

"Chan, it's okay."

"No, it's not okay. First she runs off, scaring us half to death. Then she sasses us." That was one of the few times I had heard my mother use a term like *sass*. She considered Southernisms signs of ignorance or low class. I was discouraged from using them. She did allow me to call her Mama, which was not too Southern, I guessed. Endearing, she called it.

"Chan…"

"George, she can't get away with this kind of behavior," Mama retorted.

"Since when did you become a Nazi?"

I had never heard Daddy use that tone with my mother.

"Since you abdicated your position."

"Me? I don't drag our daughter off to artist colonies all over the country."

"No, you don't. If you had your way, we'd all stay safe and sound inside the prison you built for us."

"Prison?"

"Yeah, some people call it home, but for me it's been..."

I had never heard my parents speak to each other that way, though I had been sure these kinds of discussions had indeed taken place. I was silent, listening, trying to absorb every word and every nuance, hoping they could somehow make the puzzle pieces of my life fit together.

The conversation stopped. They looked as though they realized they had gone too far, but I wanted to know more.

"Hey, by the way, I don't need a bodyguard," I quipped, hoping that would further the dialogue between my parents.

"What?" My father looked up at me.

"Malcolm."

"Malcolm?" Mama finally looked at me too.

"Yeah, you don't have to make him sleep on the floor beside me to make sure I don't run away again."

My parents looked at each other.

"I never asked Malcolm to..." Daddy tried to explain.

"Me either, but let's talk about your running away again." Mama uncurled her bronzed legs and stood up facing me. She looked surprised at first. I was surprised, too. When had I gotten as tall as my mother?

After I caught my breath, I turned back to the mirror. "Well, next time I won't trust a bunch of Jesus freaks on the beach, that's for sure."

"Now that you brought that up, I want to know where you slept all those nights. Did those Jesus freaks take you in? Give you a place to sleep just so they could…take advantage of you?"

I caught Daddy's expression reflected in the mirror next to mine. Amazement—the thought had never occurred to either of us.

"No. They gave me a hot dog and some marshmallows and…they prayed for me." I couldn't believe I was defending the very ones who had betrayed me.

"Oh, so that's it. They gave you their religion, too."

"Chan, stop!" My father stood in my defense.

I'd had enough. "What do you care what I do or who I hang out with? You're so into your painting and into that creep, Guy, that you don't even know where I am or what I'm doing most of the time." Maybe I'd said too much, but I didn't care.

It was my father then who needed to hear my honest feelings. "And you…you left me without even saying good-bye. You left a note, Daddy. Like I was the milkman or something. 'Hey, leave two gallons of skim, please.' And I have to hear from Mama that you're legally separating and I wasn't even asked how I felt about it." The tears of anger and self-pity were just behind my eyes.

"I didn't know how…" Daddy tried to interrupt. "Nothing's definite."

Mama's mouth tightened. "It didn't seem to matter to you anyway. You don't seem to care about anybody but yourself these days."

I looked around to see if anyone else was as incredulous as I at that statement. It was then that I realized that we were the only ones in the house. Jeanette had gathered Malcolm, Guy, and Maureen on the porch and was pouring lemonade into bright-colored aluminum glasses. If nothing else, Jeanette was sensitive to our need for privacy. She was talking loudly, perhaps to drown us out.

"I can't believe this." And I really couldn't believe it.

My mother sat back down on the couch and drew her legs under her with her hands on her knees. Her back straight, she looked like the black china cat that sat on our mantel at home.

My father stared at the floor.

"So, what happens now?" I finally asked. "Which prison do I live in? This one or the one in Jackson?"

Both parents started to respond, but a knock at the door stopped the conversation in its tracks.

Chapter Twenty-two

I caught a glimpse of Paul and Rachel at the front door as my father opened it. Fortunately I was near enough to my room to escape there before they saw me. I could only hear bits and pieces of the conversation, but the tone seemed somber. After a few minutes, the voices stopped, the screen door slammed, and I waited. Waiting just a bit longer to be sure, I opened the bedroom door to have a look around. Malcolm stepped into view.

"Here." Malcolm held out a folded piece of notebook paper and a large leather-bound book. I could only imagine how long Malcolm had stood outside my locked bedroom door waiting for me to come out.

"What is that?" I asked. But I already knew the answer to my question. The conversation my parents had had with the visitors was loud enough that I could tell what it was about.

"It's a note from Paul and Rachel." Malcolm stood dutifully, holding the book and the note, waiting for me to take them. Rachel. That must be Baltimore's name.

"I don't want them."

"Okay. I'll put them on the kitchen table. You can look at them later." Malcolm turned.

I slammed the door, locked it again, and threw myself on the bed. The transistor radio beside my bed had been my link to the outside world for many weeks. It had picked up not only local stations, but also one in Chicago. I had felt a little sophisticated listening to sounds from a far-off city and at that moment I tuned my radio to WGN to try to feel something like sophistication again.

"Dear Kathleen…" I had waited another ten minutes or so before I opened the door just a crack to see if anyone was nearby. The note and the book were still lying on the table where Malcolm had put them. The room was empty of people.

"We came by to explain." The note looked like it had been written by a female hand. Rachel, I guessed. "Sorry that we didn't get to speak to you directly, but we hope you'll forgive us for calling the police and telling them where you were." They could hope forever before I was willing to forgive them. "Our retreat is over today and so we have to leave. Please know that we did what we thought was the right thing for your safety and for your family. We pray that one day this will all make sense and that you'll see God's hand in it. Blessings. Rachel." Down in the left-hand corner was scrawled, "Jeremiah 31:3."

Before I was tempted to read the note again, I crumpled it and tossed it in the kitchen trashcan.

The book was heavy and I wasn't surprised to see the words *Holy Bible* engraved on the front. Also engraved in gold letters were the words "Rachel Marie Jeffries." What?

Opening the Book, I took my thumb and let the pages flutter quickly from front to back. At some point, I stopped and looked at one of the pages marked with a paper bookmark. Many of the words were underlined, and some of the pages were dog-eared. Words and phrases were written in ballpoint ink in the margins. Then it occurred to me. This was a used Book. Rachel Whoever-She-Was hadn't cared enough to bring me a new Bible. The binding on this one was bent and broken, and many of the pages were wrinkled. An air of unspeakable pity blew over me. I didn't even rate a new book. In fact, everything I had was second- or third-hand. Nothing was my own. I had tolerated hand-me-down dreams and spaces and relationships. My resolve at that moment was to find something of my own that I could control. But before I searched for that something, I tossed the hand-me-down Bible in the kitchen garbage can where I had deposited the note.

Chapter Twenty-three

The next day was unbearably hot. Even with the doors and windows shut and the window units humming, nothing could keep the hot, humid late-July air from penetrating the cabin. I took three showers that day, but within a couple of hours of drying off, I was sticky and greasy all over. I was drained of all my energy.

My father was staying in the house, sleeping on the leather couch in the living room. During the daylight hours, he spent some time on the telephone talking to someone who I guessed was connected to the bank in Jackson. At least it all sounded like business. I do not remember speaking to him during those days and I do not remember how many days he stayed. I just came to the table at mealtime, picked at my food, and then retreated to my bedroom and listened to the same records over and over. Even though we shared a room, I was able to avoid physical or verbal contact with my mother. She would brush past me exiting or entering the bathroom, but neither she nor I ever said a word. I ignored any questions or comments from Malcolm and Jeanette, and after a few days I realized my silence was contagious. Jeanette had almost completely stopped talking to the TV, and anytime she spoke to the others, it was in a half voice.

Though I had never been to one, I imagined it was like being at a funeral. Necessary pleasantries would be exchanged, but a respect for the dead and mourning was observed. I felt empowered that my attitude could have so much influence on a houseful of people. At some point I realized I hadn't seen Guy or Maureen for a few days. Had Jeanette asked them to leave the colony? Had they left on their own? Had I so wanted them to be invisible that they indeed now were? Or had they never existed? It didn't matter. I was glad they were gone.

The shrill tone of my mother's voice and the cold air of the refrigerator brought me to reality.

"Kathleen! What in the world?"

A sticky ooze had soaked my nightgown, and the sight of a creamy yellow substance on my hands was as surprising to me as it was to those who had suddenly gathered around me. Daddy, Malcolm, and Jeanette had joined my mother. I was sitting with my back against the open refrigerator door. The adults had all stooped down to my eye level and were trying to blink back their disbelief. Malcolm stood behind them looking totally shocked. I, too, was trying to take it all in; I had no idea how I had gotten to this place. Next to my foot was an empty paper egg crate, and strewn about me were shattered eggshells. My cheeks were stiff. I reached up to touch my face, and it felt like school glue had been rubbed on it. I tried to figure out what had happened and what I had been doing just prior to this discovery. From the looks of things, I had unknowingly helped myself to several raw eggs in the middle of the night while I was asleep. I felt nauseated at the thought, but I tried not to believe what I had done. I swallowed, hoping there was nothing still lingering on my palate.

Finally I spoke. Even I was amazed to hear myself say, "What are you all looking at?"

"She hasn't spoken for two weeks, hardly eaten at all, and several nights she's been walking in her sleep, sometimes raiding the refrigerator. Last night...it was a half dozen raw eggs."

It was just after eight o'clock in the morning, and already my father was on the phone. This was not bank business, however. I knew he was talking about me, but to whom I did not know. He was trying to speak softly, but with only one telephone in the cabin, it was hard for anyone to have a private conversation. I got out of bed and opened the bedroom door just a bit so I could listen. My mother was not in her bed. I figured she was standing next to my father, maybe being his lookout in case I entered the room. I just stood and listened.

"Uh huh." "Yes." "I understand." "Thank you, Doctor."

Doctor? Not only was I hearing about other sleepwalking episodes for the first time, I was discovering that I had a serious enough problem to warrant a call to a doctor. My father hung up the phone, and I jumped back to my bed, but with the door cracked slightly, I could still hear a whispered conversation between my parents.

"Drugs?" my mother said loudly enough that my father shushed her.

I had heard some kids talk about pot at the Hangout, but I hadn't even been offered any. I was about to burst into the room and defend my drug-free status when my father made my defense unnecessary.

"Temporarily," he said. "The doctor figures the trauma of her running away—or some trauma she suffered during her time away—has caused some psychological problems. Anxiety, he guesses."

"But give her pills for that?"

Daddy shushed Mama again. "The doctor said he'd call in a prescription for Valium or Librium if we wanted him to. Otherwise, he'd want to see her and run some tests, maybe have her talk to a psychiatrist."

My mother was silent for a few seconds, and then I heard her sniffing back tears. Could it be that my mother was softening? Could she possibly have recognized her own self-absorption and was now concerned for me?

"This is all your fault, George."

Then my father was silent. In fact, the entire room went silent. I waited to see if my mother would come back into the bedroom. When she didn't, I quietly crept back to the door to look. All I could see was my father sitting on the leather couch, running his fingers through his unkempt hair. Dark circles hung from his lower eyelids. I felt a twinge of pity for him. It was the first feeling I remembered having in many days. It did not feel good to let down my steely internal defenses, and so

I chose not to entertain any other thoughts of forgiveness. I forced myself not to open the door and jump into his arms. Instead, I closed and locked the door and then took out a pair of scissors from the bathroom drawer.

Chapter Twenty-four

The only reason I knew that two weeks had passed since I'd run away and been caught was that I had overheard my father tell the doctor as much. It must already have been August by then. Apparently I had been quite "out of touch" to let two whole weeks go by without realizing it. I shuddered a little bit to think what I might have done otherwise. If I had indeed been sleepwalking, what else had I done? What else had been done to me? I mentally explored several possibilities. Had my parents already given me psychotic drugs? Had Paul and Rachel somehow slipped me something that had had a delayed effect? Or had the Bible been laced with a substance that would induce religious euphoria? What made me that way and the total extent of what I did during that time will always remain a mystery.

However, I was determined not to let it happen again. I would stay awake all night if I had to, and by the time I had worked through all of this in my mind, mounds of my hair lay on the bathroom floor. I didn't recognize myself in the mirror. I was glad of that. I wanted to alter myself any way that I could, so that I didn't have to be me anymore, living my humiliating life. Suddenly the rage came back in its fullest form, and I couldn't wait to see my mother's reaction when she saw me nearly bald, or for my father to see that his raven-haired beauty was shorn almost to the scalp.

My parents' reaction was not what I had expected. My mother looked at first astonished, and then a cloud of anger swept back over her face. She did not say a word about my hair. My father gasped and then turned his back. I could see that he was covering his mouth, trying to stifle whatever horror he was feeling inside.

Jeanette and Malcolm, however, showed no such signs of restraint.

"Kath-a-leen!" I smiled when Malcolm said my name. I had finally gotten the shock response I was looking for.

"Good Lord, chile. What have you gone and done?" The sight of me seemed to give Jeanette back her voice. From that moment on she began to babble as she had before, and to no one in particular. Her muttering was a mixture of thinking out loud and chanting. "Oh my Lord. He'p her. It's me. I'm askin'." Even this pleased me, for I had apparently unleashed the curse of silence that had invaded this peculiar group of people gathered around me.

I was forced to go to a beauty shop after my own appointment with the scissors. I wasn't given a choice, but the trip was explained by Jeanette as getting my hair "evened up." The beautician did not say a word about how my hair had gotten that way, so I figured she had been coached by my mother.

"There."

She finally spun me around in the chair and gave me a hand mirror to look at the back of my head. My hair was shorter than I thought, maybe two inches total all over, but at least it was all one length.

"Just like Twiggy." The beautician smiled.

The ultra-thin British model with her heavy black eye makeup and boy-short hair had started a new trend a few years back. I had never really liked the look, but had admired Twiggy's bold fashion statements that still hadn't made their way to us in south Alabama. I tentatively touched my shorn head. I might be the first resident of Jackson to boast a Twiggy haircut. That is, if I ever got back to Jackson.

"Oh, it looks pretty, Kath-a-leen." Malcolm stared at me when I walked back in the cabin. "Really." He walked a circle around me and then smiled. I knew he was sincere. Malcolm was always honest with his feelings.

"Thank you." I smiled and went straight to my room to check out my appearance.

The bathroom had been cleaned and sanitized while I was at the beauty shop. There was not even one hair, not in the sink, in the trashcan, nor on the floor. I guessed Jeanette had removed the evidence of my tirade to somehow ease the transition back.

A timid knock on the bedroom door drew me away from the mirror on the dresser.

"What do you want, Malcolm?" I tried not to sound too annoyed.

"It's me, Bee-bee." Daddy smiled when I opened the door. "Hey, it looks great." I wasn't sure if he was placating me or not, but he sounded genuine anyway. I stepped aside to let him enter the room. He sat on the edge of the bed for a second and looked uneasy, as if he were about to tell me horrible news.

"I've got to go back to Jackson tomorrow. The bank called and said the examiners are there, and I need to go back home for a few days."

That didn't sound so horrible. "Are you coming back?"

"Oh, sure. As soon as the bank examiners are through. I've already told your grandfather I need to be here. However, the examiners..."

"That's okay, Daddy." It was the first time I had spoken kindly to my father in over two weeks.

"I'd take you back with me, but I'll be so busy at the bank, we wouldn't have much time together. Of course, you could stay with Mimi..."

"I'd rather stay here, I guess, for now." I couldn't stand to stay with my grandmother, whose disapproval of me would probably be as oppressive as my mother's, but for different reasons.

"We've got a lot of talking to do, I know. And I don't want to leave you now..."

"Daddy, don't. It's okay."

I was trying hard to act normal. Drug therapy had already been suggested, but I wondered if something even more dire could be in the works.

Chapter Twenty-five

Daddy drove away. He waved over his shoulder, but I knew it was because he had to look away to hide the tears I had seen welling up as he hugged me at the door.

Suddenly I was hungry and I knew that Jeanette had started keeping fully prepared foods in the refrigerator just for me, in case I went on an eating-and-sleeping binge again. When I opened the door to the refrigerator, I noticed that the egg carton was pushed all the way to the back. The potato salad in the small bowl in the very front was just the right portion for me.

It was dusk, but the heat and humidity sliced through me like a knife when I opened the back door to the cabin. For a few days, I had forced myself to normalcy. No one tried to herd me back inside, so I figured the rest of the household believed I was no longer a flight risk and had called off the safety vigil over me. I stood for a few seconds and caught my breath. I had figured my mother to be up on her usual dune looking over the gulf and thinking far-away thoughts. I had figured right. She almost looked pleased to see me as I walked up the sandy hill and sat down silently beside her. I wondered for a moment if she was glad to see me there or see my father go.

I thought it was a dream much like the one I had had on the beach at the beginning of my escape. I felt my mother's warm hand on my back. She rubbed my shoulder gently and then moved her hand up to my newly bobbed hair. She didn't say a word, but she threaded her long fingers through the strands of my hair and combed them upward. I didn't mind the chill bumps that gathered on my arms and legs. By the time the sun had disappeared under the horizon, I had fallen asleep in my mother's lap.

Chapter Twenty-six

M ama patted a place next to her on the leather couch. Without saying a word, she was telling me she was ready to talk. I, however, was not yet ready to talk, certainly not to talk about my behavior of the past few weeks, nor talk about my fate, which I knew would largely hinge upon my parents' decisions about their marriage.

"I'm thirsty," I responded, hoping to deflect whatever conversation we were about to have. A trip to the refrigerator might make for a more casual environment in which we could avoid the impending announcement that our family was defunct.

"Bring me some lemonade, would you?" Mama didn't seem to mind the diversion to refreshment. Jeanette always kept either ice-cold water or fresh-made lemonade in a light green oblong plastic container with a spout that hung off the metal refrigerator shelf. Whatever was put there was so tempting that it was almost impossible to pass the refrigerator without helping yourself to something cold.

I handed the glass of lemonade to my mother. I filled my own glass and tried to think of how to exit gracefully.

"Can we talk?"

I looked back at my mother. She looked small and vulnerable, and I had to answer. "Okay."

It's not like I was surprised that my mother wanted to talk to me, but I was stunned at her tone. And it was not as if this were mother talking to child, but rather woman speaking to woman. Though her opening comments sounded a bit rehearsed, I was drawn to my mother's words nonetheless.

"It's time I tell you a few things about me and your father...and you."

She had come to the University of Alabama from Baltimore, Maryland on an art scholarship. This I already knew.

My father was a dashing frat guy who came from old south money. I knew this, too.

"A friend of mine, a fellow art student, introduced me to George...your dad. He asked me to a summer rush party. I had stayed in school taking some electives through that summer before my junior year. Your father was about to be a senior.

"I had heard that George...your dad...was rich and a little bit wild. But I had been such a serious student for two years, I thought I needed some fun. And he was so cute that it wasn't like it was such a chore to go out with him." She actually giggled.

It was like I was talking to a girlfriend back home. My mother was describing my father as I would a new guy at school. I was looking at my mother for the first time as a fellow female, a regular person.

"Even though we were different as night and day, we fell in love really quickly. I went to Jackson for Labor Day. It was the first time I met your grandparents."

I had downed my lemonade and needed to go to the bathroom, but I didn't want to stop Mama from telling me the whole story.

"So? What did Papa and Mimi think of you?" I already knew the answer to the question. It was unspoken but always clear that my mother was not a favorite in-law at the Mortons'.

Mama smiled. "They liked me a lot. They were very sweet to me." Now I was confused. "Until your dad told them we were engaged."

"What did they say?"

"Well, they...weren't happy, not so much with me but that we were getting married. See, Kat, I was pregnant with you already." She said the last sentence quickly as if to minimize its impact.

Something new, but not too terribly surprising. I had heard of such things, and in my thirteen years I had come to understand how babies came to be and that it was possible that one could be conceived without benefit of wedlock. It was 1969, after all.

"Your grandparents had liked me okay when they thought I was just another one of George's flings. But when they found out I was going to be a permanent part of the family, they started finding fault with everything about me, from my Yankee upbringing to my lack of religious affiliation to my European heritage. It seemed that your grandparents' old southern charm turned sour overnight when they imagined how I would blot the family tree with all those things."

"What about me? Did they not like me either? I'm different, just like you..."

"No. You cannot think that way. I think there was natural love for their own flesh and blood that they could not deny. But I...I was somehow never accepted."

"What did you do?"

My mother was silent for a moment and then she rolled in her lips as though she were trying to swallow them.

"Have you ever wondered why you never saw any of our wedding pictures?"

It had never dawned on me.

"You mean you didn't ever get married?" My eyes grew wide. It was the only question I knew to ask.

"Yes, we got married, at the courthouse in front of a notary public. No family or friends, just some witnesses who were willing to sign the marriage certificate. Neither of our families wanted to give us a wedding."

I hadn't heard my mother mention her side of the family very often. The Asburys of Baltimore were to me only a black-and-white picture on the mantel. I had been told that we had, indeed, been to visit them on some of our New England artist jaunts early on, but for the life of me I couldn't remember them at all. I did remember, however, the call coming that my grandparents had been killed in an automobile accident. I had been in the second grade. I was left with Mimi and Papa while my parents went to the funeral. After that, I don't remember much being said about the other side of my family.

"Then what?"

"Then we went back to Tuscaloosa, where Daddy finished his degree in finance. You were born about a month before graduation."

"Did you finish college, then?" I had never heard her say.

"No. I didn't. I gave up my scholarship...and we moved to Jackson, where Daddy went to work for your grandfather at the bank."

The rest I concluded. Mimi and Papa never accepted my mother, my mother grew bitter, my father withdrew, and now all the aforementioned relationships, which had once been at least semipolite, had deteriorated, and someone wanted out. End of story.

"So, that's it?"

She paused, then sighed. "I guess." That was all she had been willing to share. It wasn't much to take in. All of this was what I had suspected it to be. So, our talk had answered very few of my questions and had replaced only some of the missing pieces. It was time to retreat again and figure this all out on my own.

Chapter Twenty-seven

It had been almost a month since I'd strolled Long Beach and stopped at the Hangout, a month since I had taken my leave of home and been turned in to the authorities by the band of religious college students.

Now, with my emotional crisis seemingly over, Mama focused on her painting again during the day. Daddy was still working with the bank examiners at home. Jeanette merrily cooked and cleaned for the remnant still at the cabin and didn't seem to be concerned with my whereabouts so much. Malcolm, however, kept a distant eye on me. I could feel it. Sometimes I would catch him looking at me, and I'd give him a warning look to which he'd blush and turn away. Occasionally I was able to escape his watch when Jeanette had him doing some household chore. Finally I found the perfect time to slip away down the beach for a couple of hours.

"Hey." Barry looked at me as though he had never seen me. I could believe that. Since my last encounter with him a month before, I had grown a little bit taller and rounder, and had cut my hair very short. I looked nothing like my former self. I smiled and was glad to reacquaint myself with him as an entirely different person.

"Hey." I tried a cool attitude this time.

"Your first time here?" Barry asked, keeping an eye on the shoreline while he tried to make conversation with me. Apparently, I really was a new face to him.

"Uh, no. I've been here before. Not in a while though."

"There's a live band coming tonight, you know? The Chimes. They're out of Dothan, I think."

"Great. What time?"

"Uh. I think they start at eight. Hope you can come." He looked back at me and shot the shocking-white-teeth smile that seemed to have gotten even whiter as his tan had grown darker.

I was pretty sure he wasn't asking me to be his date. He hadn't even asked my name. But I imagined for the next few minutes what it might be like to have a date. I needed a new alias. I needed more grown-up language. I needed clothes.

I found Mama over on the bayside. She had rigged herself a faded beach umbrella to shade her and her work from the blazing sun. She wore her wide-brimmed hat, short shorts, a halter top, and large sunglasses. She looked like a movie star trying to conceal her identity.

"Where is everybody?" I called to her from across the street.

Mama looked up and seemed surprised to see me. I wondered if she knew I had been gone for almost two hours after lunch.

"Hey. I don't know. Aren't Jeanette and Malcolm in the cabin?" she asked.

"No. Nobody's there."

"You need something?"

"No, just wondering where everybody was. I'm thinking about walking down to Alvin's just to look around."

My mother looked at me with a bit of concern. "Oh. Well, be really careful. Okay?"

Alvin's, the nearest beach shop, was a couple of blocks up on the highway. Her caution to me was about crossing the road in traffic.

"I will."

I wouldn't need much money to buy the things I had in mind, but I had stuffed about forty dollars in my shorts pocket just in case.

I spent just twenty-five dollars on a new pair of shorts, a midriff top, and sandals. End-of-the-season sales were my friends that day.

Bounding back into the cabin, I called out. "Hey! Anybody home?"

I had already seen Mama still sitting by the bay painting, oblivious to the fact that I had walked past her on the opposite side of the street on my way back. No one answered my call. It was then that I noticed a note on the table. It had been written by Jeanette, telling us she had taken Malcolm to a doctor's appointment in town, but that she would be back around five o'clock, in plenty of time to fix supper. It occurred to me that this might be the first time since we arrived there that I had been totally alone in the cabin. There had always been someone around. Of course, Jeanette was a permanent fixture there. So was Malcolm. The only time I had known those two to leave the cabin was on Sunday mornings when they went to church. Once a week or so Jeanette would drive herself to the grocery store, but usually Mama or Malcolm had been there. The other artists were long gone. I glanced at the clock. It was almost four. I had a whole hour to myself. How would I use it?

As I had expected, the refrigerator was full of food. In the front were lunch leftovers and half a watermelon covered by plastic wrap, and of course a full container of lemonade. The refrigerator was always like that. Full to the brim, making me wonder where Jeanette would find room for the groceries she bought once a week. I pulled a cold chicken leg off a plate and started to devour it. At that moment, I realized that in the two-plus months I had been at this cabin-colony, I hadn't really explored it. I knew my and Mama's room backward and forward, having spent many hours staring at the ceiling and the walls while listening to records and pondering life. The lower half of the walls of our room were white bead board. On the wall facing my bed there were eighteen vertical slats, not counting two half slats in the corners behind the door. On the adjoining wall, there were sixteen. On the wall where the bathroom door was cut, there were twelve. On the wall behind my bed, I counted twenty-four slats. Sometimes I'd subdivide them into groups of twos or threes. It passed the time and seemed to put things in order. All the walls could be divided by two, and only the sixteen-slat one was not divisible by three.

Malcolm's room was very small, almost the size of a closet. He had a twin bed, a dresser, and a rough-looking bedside table that looked like he had built it himself from an orange crate. It had been spray painted bright red.

The walls were bare except for three pictures, one of him at ten or eleven years old holding up a small fish, one of him and Jeanette that looked like it had been taken at a studio a couple of years back. There was one more picture above the bed. It was a picture of Jesus. I felt a sense of shame walking into his room. I had never been inside it before, and for some reason my breathing got a little shallow, as if I had come upon a sight that I was not meant to see. Something sacred—or was it a sense of foreboding?

The bed had a white chenille spread over it, and right next to his pillow there was a small stuffed bear that looked like it had seen better days. I imagined that Malcolm had arrived with a single toy, and when his parents had abandoned him, Jeanette had kept the toy for him. I wondered if Jeanette had told Malcolm the story I had overheard her tell my mother, about how his parents came to the colony under the guise of artistry, but had used the place as a dumping ground for their retarded child. I wanted to imagine, though, that Malcolm's mother had really loved him and had had to approve the place that they would leave him. I envisioned the mother checking out other places and finally finding this place where the kind but simple Jeanette would never have turned him away. According to Jeanette's account, Malcolm's father had been abusive, and so the mother had had to make a choice. If Malcolm's mother had truly loved him, she would not have left him anywhere but here.

The top drawer of the dresser was slightly open, and when I went to close it, I saw a glimpse of something that shocked me. There in the drawer was a book, but I wouldn't have regarded it at all if I hadn't seen the gold script on the bottom of the book: "Rachel Marie Jeffries." Without wondering if I needed permission, I opened the drawer and there it was: the secondhand Bible that Rachel from Baltimore had meant for me. I opened the drawer a little more and lifted the Bible out. It smelled of coffee grounds from its short stay in the garbage can. The note I had crumpled up had been smoothed out and placed inside the front cover. It was stained and wrinkled, but I could read the words. The Scripture reference Rachel had written for me to read was Jeremiah 31:3. I looked around the room and behind me into the living room for the first time since my invasion of Malcolm's space. I wasn't sure where to find this Jeremiah thing.

My occasional church attendance with my father and his parents had not taught me much about this Book. I had leafed through the ones that sat in the pew rack a couple of times, out of childish curiosity, but I hadn't taken much notice of the contents. There had been no pictures inside the pew Bibles, only occasional words written in red.

A paper bookmark I had seen before was still stuck between some pages in the middle of the book. Cut from construction paper, the bookmark had the words "for Kathleen" written in ink at the top. A chill came over me. I suddenly realized I had stumbled across a cosmic treasure hunt. Perhaps all the planets had aligned, and I was destined to find this item at this time. It was a sign. It was a new adventure. It was fate.

The idea that this was perhaps a treasure hunt was not original with me. I had seen a movie once about riddles in classic literature that when joined together had led the seeker to an ancient relic of historic value. I had been intrigued, but I had never expected to be on the receiving end of such a quest. This might be like someone was leaving me clues that would lead me somewhere or to something of value. After all, I didn't feel as though I had found this Book again by accident. I had to have been lead there by some force. And, of course, I was thankful for a private diversion from the late summer boredom.

I stuck my finger in front of the bookmark and threw back the pages. The words were underlined:

"The Lord hath appeared of old unto me, saying, Yea, I have loved thee with an everlasting love: therefore with lovingkindness have I drawn thee."

My first clue, but I had no idea what it meant. I turned a couple of pages and read these words underlined:

"Call unto me, and I will answer thee, and show thee great and mighty things, which thou knowest not."

I imagined this to be a complicated adventure that might help me keep my sanity until the summer was over, which was only three weeks away. I silently accepted the challenge.

I knew I couldn't keep the Bible. Malcolm would miss it, and besides, my treasure hunt wouldn't be a challenge if I didn't risk being found out. I would have to find times when Malcolm was out of the cabin and everyone else was otherwise occupied. Then I'd go back to the Bible and keep looking for clues.

When I opened the drawer wider to replace the Bible, I saw a brown paper sack. The mouth of the sack had been rolled down shut, and a rubber band wrapped around the sack to secure it. The word *privat* was scrawled across the paper bag in crayon. I laughed to myself, imaging what a boy like Malcolm might consider private. I figured it was seashells he had found on the beach, or maybe even another child's toy he had wanted to conceal from the world. The sack was light and puffy, as if it were filled with cotton. I smelled it. There was no odor. At that point, I had to open it. I was too curious and too alone not to. The clock on the living room wall said I had about thirty minutes before Jeanette and Malcolm's expected return. I wouldn't need that much time. All I had to do was slip off the rubber band and take a quick peek inside.

The bag was full of hair. I was certain it was my hair. I wasn't sure whether to be grossed out or warmed inside. I thought Jeanette had been the one to clean up the bathroom that day I had taken the scissors to my thick locks, and I had assumed that whoever had done it had disposed of the hair immediately. Who would want my hair? Apparently, Malcolm did. But why? I tried for a moment to think like Malcolm. Having never suspected one inappropriate thought to have entered his head, I had to believe he was saving my hair for me in case I ever needed it. I replaced the sack, closed the drawer, and went to my room wondering if I'd ever deserve a friend like Malcolm.

Chapter Twenty-eight

The new face at the dinner table looked very much out of place, but the person attached to the face never seemed to notice.

Mary Alice Spaulding, a woman, a lady, who was probably about the same age as my Mimi Morton, had driven up in her white Cadillac promptly at six o'clock in the evening, just in time for the meal of country-fried steak, gravy, and fluffy rice. Dressed in her off-white peddle pushers and navy-blue polka-dot blouse, she didn't seem the least bit concerned that she might spill gravy on the outfit made of what looked like pure silk. She dug into the hot biscuits and butter beans like she hadn't eaten in a week. I was almost right.

"Jeanette, I've been craving your cooking for a week. You can't get this kind of food in Miami. Too much Cuban influence." She and Jeanette laughed together as if they were spinster sisters. I couldn't imagine Mrs. Spaulding with her fancy car, her refined speech, and her expensive clothes (right down to the Pappagallo shoes) having anything in common with Jeanette Hudspeth, whose faded cotton Dollar Store muumuu had six food stains that I could see and no telling how many I couldn't. However, the women were as comfortable with each other as any two people I'd ever known.

The visit from the colony's benefactor apparently had not been a surprise to Jeanette or Malcolm or even to my mother. No one had informed me, however, that we would be dining with our sponsor. In fact, no one had bothered to tell me that we even had a sponsor. I guess I had always assumed that the many artist colonies we had lived in had been funded by my parents. I had never guessed that my mother's art ventures had been of any account to anyone outside the family, especially not to a lady as elegant as Mrs. Spaulding.

I listened to the lady speak to see if I could detect an accent, but there was no drawl of old south in her voice for sure, and her tone wasn't flat as a New Englander's either. She was from a place I could not define. She had mentioned Miami, but she had talked as if there were other places she resided.

"Chan, how's George?"

My face must have shown astonishment, because my mother glanced at me with a stern look. Until that moment I had never suspected that Mama had known this lady before, nor that this lady had been acquainted with my father.

"He's fine, Mary Alice. He'll be coming down here next week to finish out the summer with us."

That was news to me. I forked rice into my gaping mouth.

"And his mother?" Mrs. Spaulding scooted the remainder of the gravy on her plate to the biscuit in her hand.

"Same," my mother answered, never looking up.

I must have looked dumbfounded at this incongruent sight because Jeanette kept reminding me to eat before the food got cold. I stared at this woman across the table until even she noticed it.

"Now, Kathleen, I'm sure you don't remember me." Mrs. Spaulding sat back in her chair and wiped her hands on a paper towel that had been set beside her plate. I was embarrassed that our benefactor had no proper napkin with which to wipe her perfectly manicured fingers.

"But I remember you," she continued. "I've practically watched you grow up. Pictures mostly. It's hard to believe you're already thirteen years old."

"Uh huh." I shook off my gaze and tried to form intelligible words. "My birthday was in April."

"I know. Time flies. When my husband got so sick, we weren't able to visit all of our colonies like we had at one time. For several years, Walter couldn't travel and I just couldn't leave him, so we did most of our visiting by telephone and through the mail."

I wanted to ask about Walter and about her other colonies, but I wasn't sure it was polite. I looked at Mama for a cue.

"We were so sorry to hear about Walter's death, Mary Alice. He was just a fine man and a wonderful patron of the arts," my mother interjected sincerely. That answered one question.

"Thank you, Chandler. He loved your work so much, and our collection of Asbury-Mortons shall always remain in our gallery in South Beach."

First, that was the first time in a while I had heard anyone call my mother by her full name, and second, I hadn't ever imagined my mother's paintings to be galleried anywhere. My mother smiled and nodded.

"So, Malcolm, you've been awfully quiet tonight. What have you been up to?"

Malcolm blushed a little bit and when he smiled the deep dimple in his cheek appeared. "I went to the doctor today."

"You did?" Mrs. Spaulding said in a playful tone.

"Uh huh." Malcolm nodded.

"Yes ma'am," Jeanette corrected him.

"Yes ma'am. I got a sucker."

I, apparently, was the only one who hadn't known this woman of means as an intimate friend. Even Malcolm seemed to have had a connection with her. As the pecan pie and coffee were served, the conversation stayed light and familiar, and I watched with delight as Mrs. Spaulding and the others exchanged stories about other times they had been together.

"I'd say, 'Let's go out on the porch,' but we'd all sweat like pigs in this heat," Jeanette said, wiping her forehead with a dish towel she lifted from her lap.

"Now, Jeanette, you know that southern ladies don't sweat. They glow." Mrs. Spaulding laughed.

"Huh, then I must not be no southern lady, 'cause I sweat!" Everybody at the table laughed except me. I was embarrassed again at the crude environment that had been provided for Mary Alice Spaulding.

"It's okay. I might just go back in the bedroom for a while and write a few letters before turning in anyway. That drive from Miami is drain-ing," the lady said, pushing her chair away from the table and helping to take the dishes to the sink.

"Yeah, that drivin's a bugger," Jeanette answered. I wondered if Jeanette had ever driven outside of Bay County. "Now, Mary Alice, you let me handle them dishes. I might even warsh 'em in the morning. I don't know. You go on back and rest up. We've got a few days to talk."

The sun was almost down and I was wondering what to do next. I had been thinking all day about Barry at the Hangout, The Chimes and my new clothes. I was relieved to hear Mama say she wanted to catch the sunset, which meant she would be painting for an hour or so before it got too dark. I figured I could sneak out for a little while and try to pass myself off as a hip beachcomber. Malcolm was nursing a summer cold and had been lethargic the past few days. He was spending more time on the couch watching cartoons or whatever, but without his usual play-ful laughter at his favorite character, Popeye. I had felt a little sorry for him, but his being preoccupied would be a good thing for me.

The music was so loud that I was sure that it could be heard for miles, and I wondered how long it would be before the renters nearby would complain.

I tugged at my midriff top that was trying to roll up every time I bent over. I pulled at the short shorts, too, and smoothed them down the front before I stepped off the dark beach into the light of the dance hall.

I was about to speak to Barry, who was standing just inside the door to the open-air dance floor, when a shapely, tanned blonde girl who looked about five years older than I approached him with a smile. He greeted her with a kiss on the lips and an arm around her tiny waist.

"Oh well," I said to myself. Barry obviously already had a date, but there were so many other guys standing around the dance floor who looked unattached that I vowed not even to regard Barry unless he spoke to me first. Since it would be impossible to carry on a conversation over the loud music, I chose to sit on the dance floor windowsill instead of on the bench underneath it. There I could listen to the music and watch the people. It was slightly cooler on the sill because of a breeze that blew from the gulf. Most of the other people had learned that, too, and so they sat in the window openings, using the benches as footstools. Surprisingly, I found a corner unoccupied and leaned my back against it. I swung one leg up on the sill and admired my new sandals.

The band was loud, but it was pretty good by my standards. They were playing an Otis Redding song, "Sittin' On the Dock of the Bay" that to me sounded a lot like the record. I wasn't sitting on a dock, and I wasn't looking at the bay, but the fact that I was hearing that song and looking out over the Gulf of Mexico was a comfort, as if I were supposed to be there.

Three guys who looked to be in their twenties came and occupied the space next to me in the windowsill. I removed my leg to give them plenty of room. One of the guys had longer hair. It was shaggy and windtossed. His face, except for his forehead, was badly sunburned, especially his nose. Anyone who knew the beach knew better than to get that burned, so I figured this guy was from up north somewhere. He wore shorts, and his legs were white as a sheet underneath the matted hair, but his long, thin forearms were dark pink.

The three guys yelled in each other's ears during the loud music, but I couldn't hear their conversation. That is, until the music ended and I heard one of them yell, "Woodstock."

The Chimes guitar player and the drummer played a quick vamp while the lead singer announced that the band would be taking a short break.

The three guys sitting next to me didn't move, nor did I. I thought this might be an interesting conversation to follow and to learn from.

I had heard about the upcoming music festival, Woodstock, that would be held in the state of New York. I had heard some talk of it on TV over the past few days. I knew I wouldn't be attending, but the more I listened, the more I realized that these three sitting next to me were making their plans to go.

"You guys going up for Woodstock?" The question sneaked out of my mouth somehow.

The three men looked at me in unison. It was then that I noticed the other two. The one in the middle had thick black hair all over his face except for his eyes and nose. The mustache, beard, and sideburns made one continuous loop under his chin to a wild mop of coarse hair on his head. I couldn't even see his mouth until he spoke.

"Yeah. You?" He smiled a bit, and I could see he actually had teeth and lips. He leaned forward, resting his elbows on his knees, which were covered by ragged blue jeans. I could see a tattoo on his right upper arm. It was a leaf of some kind.

"Maybe. I haven't decided." I tried to deepen my voice. My mind was also trying to conjure up a new identity in case these men asked about me. I considered the Baltimore cover and the name Marcy, my newest fantasy name for myself, if I needed it.

The third guy leaned forward then, and I could see that he was the best looking of the three, with dishwater-blond hair that was cropped neatly just below his ears. He wore threadbare khaki pants that were frayed and gray with dirt on the bottom. He wore no shoes. He wore no shirt, either, except a kind of vest that looked like he had cut it out of an old jacket. The vest had a hand-painted peace symbol on the back. His blond chest hair poked out of the vest, and I tried not to stare at his tanned, muscular arms. The sunburned guy spoke for the first time, and I could detect an accent. Maybe British.

"Well, love. We've got a van and there's an empty space for a bird like you." The chest-hair guy smiled again, this time a little friendlier.

"Uh, well…" There were two pieces of information I didn't want to give away. One, I was only thirteen years old. Two, I had run away once and was sure I would be sent to jail or to the state mental hospital if I tried it again. "I have my own van. Thanks though."

"That's groovy, love. It's groovy."

By that time in my life I was more informed, more aware of my world. I even knew what the term *hippie* meant. They were people who had thrown out all traditional values and had started "doing their own thing." They liked flowers and nature and drugs. They were antiwar and anti-jobs and seemed to love music, especially songs about peace. I remembered times when my mother had been referred to as a hippie, but in my eyes she did not fit the profile. However, at that moment, it dawned on me that these three might, but I was disappointed that I could never tell anybody about this encounter, at least not for a while.

The guys talked among themselves, mentioning names like Jimi Hendrix and Joe Cocker. They talked about groups that sounded familiar: Creedence Clearwater Revival, The Who, Grateful Dead, and Jefferson Airplane. I hadn't ever asked, but I was sure my parents wouldn't let me buy their records.

Finally the blond guy on the end held up two fingers and flashed the charming smile at me. "Peace," he said, and the three stood and walked away just as the band came back to the makeshift stage and started tuning for the next set.

I was both amused and impressed with myself that I had crossed over my own cultural roots, at least in conversation, and I longed for more such experiences. Those would have to wait, though. I needed to get back to the cabin before anyone knew I was gone.

The next day I was able to slip away down to Alvin's where there was a newsstand in the back. The latest issues of *Fave*, *Tiger Beat*, and *16* had just come out, and I was ready to see what was new in the teen idol world, but also to see if there was anything about the big upcoming music event. It had occurred to me that the brief encounter I had had the night before with the Woodstock-bound hippies might actually have been a brush with fame. What if those guys were in a band? What if they were famous rockers and I didn't even know it? All I had followed were the bands like The Monkees, Herman's Hermits, and Paul Revere and the Raiders. These certainly wouldn't have been in the lineup for Woodstock. Too cheeky. Too white bread. The guys I had met at the Hangout looked to be serious about the music, so I looked furiously through the magazines hoping to find a familiar face. If the guys had been famous rock musicians, I would have a story to tell for years to come.

The articles and pictures in the magazines were mostly of Bobby Sherman, Davy Jones, and the Cowsills. I would check again next month, after the festival, to see if I could recognize any of my new acquaintances, but I knew that my chance of having brushed that near to fame was possible. It was another fantasy that I could create that might make the long, hot August days ahead bearable. But when my father showed up a few days later, I had a new distraction and a new obstacle to my treasure hunt.

Chapter Twenty-nine

The presence of our Mrs. Spaulding and my father was both a blessing and a curse. A blessing because everyone seemed to be focused on Mrs. Spaulding's needs, even though she never demanded it. After his warm greeting to me, my father spent much of his time talking with Mary Alice, reminiscing, as if they had been old and fast friends. I didn't mind though. Because of this I was able to slide under the radar and elude even the watchful eye of Malcolm. Their presence was a curse because the cabin was rarely vacant, and therefore my treasure hunt sessions using the Bible in Malcolm's dresser were limited to brief, stolen moments. I figured I could slip the book out for a couple of hours at a time when no one was around and then steal a moment later to slip it back into the drawer before Malcolm noticed. I waited until Malcolm was out of the house doing something with Jeanette and everyone else was engaged in something else before I tried.

I took the Book with me into the bathroom. That was about the only place I could be left alone, undisturbed, for several minutes at a time. Starting at the bookmarked place, I reread the underlined words.

"The Lord hath appeared of old unto me, saying, Yea, I have loved thee with an everlasting love: therefore with lovingkindness have I drawn thee."

"Call unto me, and I will answer thee, and show thee great and mighty things, which thou knowest not."

Before I went further, I tried to decipher the messages I had just read. This was definitely old literature. Thee. Knowest. These were like some of the Shakespearean works we had read in Miss Early's English class. The teacher had made us read aloud the passages, even memorize and recite some. To a preadolescent, this could be the most embarrassing moment of life, or at least the most memorable. Once a boy named Johnny was reciting from the play "Julius Caesar." Johnny was from a poor farming family and barely passed each grade with me. He always wore overalls and hard-soled shoes that were too large for him. I don't remember seeing him dressed any other way. Johnny was quiet, almost detached, but Miss Early was determined that all of us would memorize and recite some of the classic drama. It was Johnny's turn to stand at the front of the room to quote the character Mark Antony. The first time I think I ever heard him speak, he said in a true hillbilly brogue, "Fran-inds, Romans, countr'men. Lend me yo' years." The giggle started at the back of the room and worked its way forward. I had felt sorry for Johnny but hadn't wanted to show it to my peers, so I laughed, too. Later, I was sorry I had. We all were eventually. The next summer, Johnny was thrown from a horse and died instantly from a broken neck. I didn't go to the funeral, but someone told me it was the saddest thing they'd ever seen.

At that moment I tried to imagine Johnny saying the ancient words I was reading, but somehow I felt that these were not words to be taken lightly. I wrote them down in a spiral notebook so I could study them later.

I took a moment to leaf through the pages of the entire book. Many of the pages had notes in the margins, some like personal notes to herself. "Rach, remember this" was written beside these words underlined under the heading "Lamentations":

"It is of the Lord's mercies that we are not consumed, because his compassions fail not. They are new every morning: great is thy faithfulness."

I remembered Mr. Bowman, the science teacher, again because these were words that he might say and or even might have said. Mercy. Compassion. Faithfulness. Words from the Bible that Mr. Bowman had slipped into his lectures had mostly slipped past me. Maybe, I thought, this was part of the search I was being drawn into.

I wrote down the new clues I had found and was able to slip the Bible back into Malcolm's drawer. And just in time.

"Scat!" I heard Jeanette say, right after Malcolm sneezed. I saw the two coming back into the kitchen from the back porch and was pretty sure they hadn't seen me.

∞

"Hey everybody, dinner's on me. We have a reservation at the Paradise Restaurant at six." It was an edict announced by Mrs. Spaulding.

In her days at the colony, Mary Alice Spaulding had practically taken over. Though Jeanette retained her cooking duties, our benefactor insisted on doing everything else. She bought groceries, she cleaned, and she took care of Malcolm, whose cold did not seem to be getting better. His cough was in his bronicals, Jeanette declared, and it seemed to frighten her. Mrs. Spaulding drove Malcolm to his doctor's appointments and would fetch prescription medicines from the drugstore.

"What did the doctor say?" Jeanette asked as Mrs. Spaulding and Malcolm walked into the door after his second appointment in two days.

"Well, let me give Malcolm the first dose of this medicine, and then we'll talk," Mary Alice answered as she ushered Malcolm into his room and pulled down the covers.

I could see and hear everything from my bed, and I was interested enough to look up from my newest *Fave* to listen to what was going on.

Mrs. Spaulding came out of Malcolm's bedroom and closed the door. Jeanette, I guessed, was sitting at the table just outside my line of sight. I could hear her rattling ice in her aluminum glass of something cold, probably lemonade. I turned on my back and held the magazine up toward the ceiling. I pretended not to notice the others in the next room.

The voices got quiet and I had to strain to hear.

"There's a doctor at Ochsner's in New Orleans who can see him in a few days. He's a specialist in these kinds of things." Mrs. Spaulding sounded calm.

Jeanette sounded worried. "But what can they do for him?"

I sensed there was something quite serious going on with Malcolm, more serious than the common cold.

"This doctor is a pioneer in fixing heart defects with surgery. He was trained at Minnesota. After looking at Malcolm's charts, this doctor seems to think he can repair that valve."

"Surg'ry?" Jeanette sounded on the verge of tears.

"Now, Jeanette, before you ask, don't worry about the money. Whatever Malcolm needs, we will provide."

I wondered who else was involved in the *we* she spoke of.

"But what if it doesn't work, or sumpin' goes wrong? He's all I've got, Mary Alice." It was sad to think that a flawed child that wasn't even her own could be all that she had. I was also struck by the familiar way in which Jeanette addressed Mrs. Spaulding. It was then that Jeanette launched into a full sob. Though I couldn't see them, I could imagine Mrs. Spaulding pulling Jeanette to her in a kind embrace.

Their conversation was sobering. Though I had begun to suspect that Malcolm's illness was more serious than just a cold, I'd had no idea he was suffering from a heart condition. I wondered what to say or if I could help in any way. My parents had gone out for a while, and I didn't even have my mother to talk this over with. Then I realized I still had the Bible that was supposed to be hidden in Malcolm's top drawer. I had taken it when he and Mrs. Spaulding had driven off and had vowed to keep reading through it while they were gone. However, I had decided to read an article about David Cassidy instead, so I had stashed the Bible under the bed for the time being. Just as I was about to retrieve it, I heard the front door open and my parents' voices.

"What's going on?" my dad asked.

"Jeanette, is everything all right?" my mother added.

I was now the only resident at the colony not in the loop, except for

Malcolm, so I dismounted my bed and went into hear the news that Malcolm's heart valve needed to be repaired or he might die.

"The doctor wants him to get over this cold before they do anything," Mrs. Spaulding explained. "But the doctor's not sure if this is just a cold either. Bacteria could be causing his lung congestion, and if so, surgery would be risky. They've started him on some new antibiotic to see if it clears up soon." I must have let out an audible sigh of relief because everyone in the room turned and looked at me.

"Hey, Bee-bee." My father reached out to me, and I allowed him to cradle me under his arm.

"I didn't know Malcolm was that sick," I said.

"Well, hon, we've known for a long time that Malcolm had a heart defect, a valve that wasn't right when he was born." Such a simplistic answer was what I would expect from Jeanette, but it seemed to be all I could understand myself.

"What can we do?" Mama asked.

"We'll wait a few days, and if he gets better with this new medicine, we'll go over to New Orleans and see this specialist." It was another one of Mrs. Spaulding's edicts, and it was the final word on the subject for that day.

Chapter Thirty

It became the family vacation we had never had. For days, my father, my mother, and I covered every attraction the beach had to offer. First, we played Goofy Golf, and since I made a hole in one on the last hole (a huge colorful fish with its mouth opened), I got a free game. I was certain we would return to redeem my free-game card later. But there was so much more to do than play Goofy Golf. We road the Starliner roller coaster several times. The rides were fifty cents apiece, and if there wasn't a long line waiting, you could re-ride for a quarter. I think we rode eight times in a row. The best part was seeing my parents doing something together. Though they took turns riding in the two-man car with me, never together, I was hopeful this would be the beginning of their reconciliation. I was so busy reveling in this recreation time with all three of us that I was hardly aware of any tension or affection my mother and father may have shown each other. For a few days, however, my mother seemed to forget her painting except for the occasional comment about the colors of the sunset. My father didn't mention the bank even once. And I said nothing about the precarious state of their marriage for fear this bliss would disappear.

"Let's go to Shell Island tomorrow," my dad said as we were sitting at the A&W across from Long Beach.

"Shell Island?" I mumbled through the last bite of my foot-long hot dog. For a few seconds I was reminded of the mouth-stuffing episode I'd had at the campfire with the Jesus freaks.

"Yeah, it's a wildlife preserve they've just opened to the public. You can take a boat out there and see dolphins and other marine life," Daddy answered. "I think they'll let you snorkel, too. I can get some gear, and we can see the fish up close." I wasn't sure about that. But I was more troubled by the sudden "up" tone of my father's voice. It was foreign to me, and it sounded forced.

"And what about the Gulfarium?" Mama added. "We haven't been there either."

I wanted to add that we hadn't been anywhere at all during our months there, but there seemed to be a spell over us that I didn't want to break.

I admitted to myself that I had missed Jeanette's cooking during those days. My parents and I had been dining on seafood and fast food and sodas, which normally I would have preferred, but there was always something about the meals that were prepared at the colony that had a personal touch. I apparently had been overcome with sentimentality.

We had gone to Shell Island, and on the way back to the cabin I asked from the backseat, "So, where to tomorrow?" I asked, sounding surprisingly chipper.

"Well…" My father looked at my mother, who returned his gaze. My heart sank. I knew this was the end of our idyllic adventure, and I silently chided myself for making it end.

"We could go back to Goofy Golf, if you'd like," my mother said matter-of-factly. Maybe I had misread the body language and the looks at each other. Over my thirteen years, I had tried to learn to read such subtle things, and as I had gotten older, I'd tried filling in the blanks that unspoken cues could not describe.

"We don't have to do anything. I mean, I was just asking."

My father smiled. "We've kind of packed a lot of stuff into three days, haven't we?"

"Yeah," I mumbled. I debated for a minute or two whether to broach the subject of when or if we were returning to Jackson. After all, school would be starting back soon, and so far no one had even mentioned that fact. By the tenth of the month in other Augusts, we had already gone to Montgomery or Mobile and shopped for new school clothes and supplies. It was a subject that would have to be discussed, but I wasn't sure if this was the right moment. By the time I decided I would mention where I'd be spending the upcoming school year, we were pulling into the driveway at the cabin. A familiar black Cadillac with Alabama number 16 plates sat in the driveway. I knew from the number it was from Clarke County, where Jackson is located, and I knew from years of being in my family who the car belonged to. I had not heard that my grandmother would be visiting us, and when I saw my parents' surprise at Mimi's presence, I realized I wasn't the only one that hadn't been told.

"There you are," Mimi said as we walked in the door. She said it as if we were late for an appointment with her.

"Mom, what you doing here?" my father asked.

"We didn't know you were coming, Margaret," my mother added. Hearing my grandmother's first name was a little bit of a shock. I couldn't remember ever hearing my mother regard Mimi in this way. Mama had almost always referred to her as "your grandmother" when speaking to me. Hardly ever had my mother called my grandmother by the grandchildren's pet name for her.

Before I could greet her or she me, Mimi put her hands on her hips. "Child, what have you done to your hair?" I realized this was the first time my grandmother had seen me with my Twiggy cut.

"Uh…"

"Doesn't it look cute?" A voice in the background sounded as if it was trying to rescue me. I could tell it was Mary Alice Spaulding.

My grandmother was not turned in her tone. "It looks…okay. You look a lot older, I guess." Mimi couldn't have said anything more complimentary than that.

Again, Mrs. Spaulding interjected. "You probably don't know this, Kathleen, but your grandmother and I go way back. Back to Tri-Delt days."

"Tri what?" I asked as Mrs. Spaulding stepped out of the shadows of the kitchen into the light of the main room.

"Tri-Delt. Delta, Delta, Delta. We were in the same sorority at Alabama many years ago," Mrs. Spaulding offered. My grandmother was still gazing at my short haircut, approaching me now and then and running her fingers through the hair on the back of my head.

"Oh. I didn't know that." During my days at this artist colony, I learned many things, some of which I had longed to discover and others I wished I'd never found out.

It was then that I saw Dorothy step from one of the bedrooms. She was wiping her hands on her apron. Dorothy smiled at me and I smiled back, but we did not exchange greetings. Though slavery had long been abolished in the Deep South by 1969, it was quite common for white families, even those who were not so wealthy, to employ a black person or two. Gardeners, maids, drivers. My grandparents usually employed seven or more black people, and Dorothy had been their cook for as long as I could remember. I was glad to see her, but then I became aware that Jeanette was not puttering around the kitchen as usual.

Suddenly I was worried. Malcolm's bedroom door was closed, and I feared that something had happened to him.

Before anyone else spoke I had to get one piece of information. "Where is Malcolm?"

Chapter Thirty-one

The cabin was full again. Actually it was overfull. Mama and I still occupied our "suite," the only room with two beds and a bath. Jeanette stayed in her small room and shared a bathroom with Malcolm. Mrs. Spaulding had taken the single room with a bath that Guy had vacated, and my grandmother took the other room and bath where Maureen had stayed for a couple of months. Dorothy, however, was to sleep on the screened-in porch that faced the gulf. Ordinarily that would have been nice, even preferable, since there was a moderately comfortable hammock out there, and the gulf's purr at night would have lulled anybody to sleep. But then, in mid-August, the temperature hardly ever got down below the mid-80s even in the middle of the night, and with the humidity, I imagined it could not be anything but miserable. Dorothy didn't seem to mind. Like so many of the other black people who worked for my grandparents, she was content to be working and receiving a better than average wage. She probably looked upon her trip to the beach as a treat rather than a work assignment.

By the next day, Malcolm was up and around, although he still had a nasty cough. Apparently the medicines had helped him, and I was curious as to what might happen next.

"Mama, is Malcolm going to have that surgery now?" I asked after breakfast while we were getting dressed for the day.

"Probably. We're waiting on a call from the specialist in New Orleans. When they have an opening, Malcolm and Jeanette and maybe Mary Alice will drive over there, and they'll run some tests first. Then perhaps the surgery."

"So, that's why Dorothy's here? To cook and clean in case Jeanette has to go with Malcolm?"

"Yes, that's right." Mama answered.

"So, why is Mimi here?" I dared to ask.

"That's a good question." End of conversation.

After Mama left the room, I remembered I'd hidden the Bible under my bed, and I wondered if Jeanette or Dorothy had found it when they were cleaning. I squatted by my bed and looked. It was still there. Then I wondered if Malcolm had missed it. Then I wondered why I was so concerned about Malcolm missing it. It had been given to me, after all, and he had just rescued it and was keeping it safe for me. I decided to continue my treasure hunt. I had left the bookmark with my name on it in the last place I had read, and so I started there.

"It is of the Lord's mercies that we are not consumed, because his compassions fail not. They are new every morning: great is thy faithfulness."

I wondered what mercies were and if I could find a new one that morning. I filed the thought away and vowed to remind myself to look for that kind of clue. The Bible went between my mattress and box spring this time.

I had gotten a five-year diary on my tenth birthday, and I had written a few things in it that I considered now to be juvenile, but I had seen it lying in the box of toys, books, and records that my mother had packed for me at the beginning of the summer. I thought this might be a good time to begin again recording the events of my days. There was much that had already happened during the summer that I had stored only in my mind. I felt compelled to write down not only events, but feelings as well. It was a teenage thing. The diary was in the bottom of the box next to Mrs. Beasley.

Mrs. Beasley didn't look at all happy to see me. Her painted-on expression was still pleasant, but still vacant. However, when I lifted her out of the box to get to my diary, she seemed to perk up just a bit. I decided to emancipate her from the closet box and let her live under the bed.

The diary was where I had remembered it. It was locked, and the keys bulged from behind the back cover. I slid my fingers down between the cover and last page and pulled out two keys tied together with a red ribbon. I was suddenly aware that my diary would have been just as simple for someone else to have opened. I didn't remember writing any intimate thoughts or deep secrets in those pages. Still, a diary should be private, I thought.

It only took me a few minutes to read what I had already written.

April 25: "I got this diary from my friend, Karen, for my tenth birthday."

I remembered the party. My parents had rented out the recreation center in Jackson, and I had been able to invite thirty or so kids to the party. With the rental of the center, everybody got free skates. However, many children brought their own. It had been hard to get the boys to stop skating long enough to watch me blow out the candles on the cake and open my presents. I had expected as much. However, when it was announced that the cake and ice cream were about to be served, the skating floor cleared, and hungry boys and girls lined the rink with paper plates full of yellow cake with pink-and-green icing (my favorite) and mounds of vanilla ice cream.

I read on.

April 26: "Went to Mimi and Papa's house for a family birthday party."

All the cousins my age that had been at the skating party had returned the following night for the family version. I didn't get any other presents that night, except for the traditional card with fifty dollars in it from Mimi and Papa.

Dorothy had made a birthday cake, a pound cake. Dorothy had never had much luck with layer cakes. They all seemed to lean or fall or crack in the middle. "Too much Crisco," she'd declare. I always thought it was because she never used a written-down recipe. After several years of failures, she finally decided to make foolproof pound cakes in the round pan with a hole in the middle. Since it was hard to decorate a cake with a hole, Dorothy would cut out a cardboard paper disc just larger than the hole, put it on top of the cake and put icing over it. The Morton children all knew that the disc was there, and it was declared that the birthday boy and girl, or the son or daughter of the birthday adult, would receive the disc and get to lick all the icing off of it. It was a tradition at the Morton family birthday parties, one I wondered whether I'd ever experience again.

May 30: "Packing to go with Mama to North Carolina."

That was all I had written for many pages. Apparently after that we had spent the summer in the mountains, and I had not packed my diary. Or maybe I had packed it and just not found anything noteworthy about North Carolina.

September 3: "Started back to school. Fifth grade. Mrs. Smith is nice. I am in the first reading group."

"The first reading group" was a distinction that was not supposed to be talked about among the children so as not to make the kids in the lower groups feel inferior. But it was a distinction that we in the top reading group used often to snub those in the second and especially those in the third reading groups. We hardly ever picked the third-groupers for dodgeball, reasoning that anybody who was a slow reader would be a slow dodger as well. The second group might get picked on a later round starting with the small wiry boys who could move fast. It was political for sure, and I was not particularly proud of my participation in it.

The following year the reading group distinctions were removed. Some mother claimed it was discrimination against her child, who bore a stigma because of it. It was a valid argument. I didn't care one way or the other. Since I was always in the first reading group, I never felt the power of bias. That same year, however, I had been annoyed to have to slow my own reading progress to accommodate the third-groupers. After sixth grade, reading groups were no longer a practice anyway, but cliques had already been formed by then, and mostly they followed the reading group lines of old.

August 11, 1969: I began a new entry with my newfound hand-writing techniques. Long curvy letters, i's dotted with open circles or maybe hearts, and I had learned to sometimes accentuate a name by writing it in puffy, connected letters. The letters, then, could be filled with multi-colored diagonal lines or whatever I chose.

The spaces in the diary designated for each day had to be divided into five sections, one for each year, so I had to conserve space. Puffy letters would not be used and curvaceous letters would have to be compressed to fit.

"Dear Diary: It's Monday. Malcolm is feeling better, so I guess he'll be having a heart operation soon."

I wondered if in years to come when I read this entry I would even remember who Malcolm was.

"Mimi is here. So is Dorothy (to cook). Still not sure what Mama and Daddy are going to do. They seem to be getting along just fine, but I know that could crash any moment."

That was all the space I had on the lines given, but I drew a tiny, puffy flower in the margin.

Chapter Thirty-two

Every time the phone rang, everybody in the cabin jumped. I know I did. We were all sure that the call coming in was from the New Orleans doctor and that Malcolm was being summoned to the hospital. By then, I had asked and been told that the surgery was risky and that it was being considered as a last resort.

The call that came in that mid-morning was for my father. It was the bank; I could tell by listening to his end of the conversation, and I feared he'd be called away again on business. However, the call ended, and he went back to the leather couch and continued reading a book. Everyone else had already gone back to whatever she was doing before. I, too, retreated to my bed for a few minutes. Finally, it seemed like the right time.

"Daddy," I spoke quietly, hoping not to disturb anyone.

"Yes, Bee-bee." My father put down his book, swung his legs to the floor, and sat upright in one fluid motion.

"Don't mean to disturb you."

"It's okay. What's up?"

I craned my neck to see what book my father was reading. "*Androm...*"

"*Andromeda Strain*. A brand-new science fiction book. It's pretty good."

My father was a science fiction fan, and he was the only one in the house who would watch *Star Trek* on TV. My mother dismissed that kind of show as farcical. She announced that she would rather look at real things, things that existed, and she would often launch into a verbal dissertation about the beauty that can be found in nature. Though she maintained her agnosticism, she was willing to regard how magnificent the world was and that whoever created it had to be a genius.

"So?" My dad opened the door to further discussion as I sat beside him on the couch.

"Nothing. Just thinking."

"About what?"

"I don't know. School." I hoped it would be enough of a conversation starter.

"Yeah, it'll be starting here pretty soon. Eighth grade, huh?"

"Yeah."

There was a pause in which I figured my father's mental wheels were turning to figure out how to tell me what my future would be.

"Well. I guess I'm not speaking out of turn. Your mother and I wanted to tell you together." He looked around the room. I wondered whether he was looking for permission or help. "Just in case you were wondering, we're all going back to Jackson together."

"Really?" I meant to restrain my childish exuberance, but it was too late.

"Yeah, we're going home next week."

"Daddy, are you serious?" I slammed my arms down onto the hard leather couch.

"Yes," my father answered, but somehow I knew that the whole deal was not done.

"And…are we all going to live in our old house…together?"

"I hope so." He spoke tentatively.

The phone rang, and everybody in the residence came out of the woodwork again to either answer it or listen to whoever did.

Jeanette, despite her size, could move pretty fast when she wanted to.

"Hello?" She caught it on the second ring.

"Yes? This is Jeanette Hudspeth." "Yes." "When?" Jeanette started waving her arms around, and somehow we got the hint that she needed a pencil and a piece of paper. When Mary Alice Spaulding produced one of each, Jeanette asked the other person on the phone to repeat the information as she wrote it down. "Thank you. Thank you very much. We'll be there."

"Well?" Mrs. Spaulding was the first to ask.

"The doctor can take him on Thursday of this week. Thursday…uh, the fourteenth."

No one knew whether to applaud or cry. It was a fact that the surgery brought many risks. It was also a fact that Malcolm needed it to live.

It was late afternoon, about the time that those inclined to napping were starting to rouse. No one was beginning supper preparations yet, but I saw my mother and Mrs. Spaulding out on the porch. Mrs. Spaulding's appearance had taken a more casual turn over those days. She wasn't wearing silk as before. Mostly breathable cotton. Her perfectly coiffed hair, which she had dubbed "limp as a fish," was usually tied up in a bandanna. The tasteful makeup she had worn at her arrival had gone by the wayside. She laughed that it would "slide right off in this heat." Still, she was elegant to me. Poised and refined, Mary Alice Spaulding reminded me somewhat of my mother. It was no wonder that the two women had spent a lot of time together since the elder lady had arrived.

Mama dabbed at a canvas while Mrs. Spaulding sat in a rocking chair and stared out at the gulf. Since the heat and humidity had increased, we no longer left the doors open between the kitchen and the screened-in porch. Earlier it had been a great place to eavesdrop on Jeanette and my mother, but now I could only see who was on the porch and not hear much of anything. I crouched behind the kitchen cabinets as I had done before. Slowly I peeked out over the counter top right behind where Mama and Mrs. Spaulding were sitting. I tried to read their lips and their body language. They did not seem to be engaged in a serious conversation, which disappointed me. There were some things that needed explaining, and I wasn't sure I would get a straight answer if I asked. I figured I would need to get that information the way I had gotten many things that summer. Steal it.

"Kath-a-leen?"

I froze. Then I instinctively tried to cover my strange behavior by opening the cabinet nearest to me.

"Hey. I was just looking for something." I stood up, pretending not to have found what I allegedly had been looking for.

"Oh," Malcolm said, appeased with my explanation. He coughed. "I'm gonna get a operation, you know."

I knew. "Yes. Are you scared?" I leaned against the counter and looked at him. I was really interested in his response.

He did not hesitate. "No. Not a bit. God will take care of me."

I was touched by his sincerity, but skeptical of his surety. "Yeah, I guess He will."

Malcolm smiled for the first time in days. His eyes still looked a little weak, but the dimple returned to its usual depth.

"Kath-a-leen, you'll pray for me, won't you, while I'm gettin' my operation?"

How could I refuse? "Of course I will." I wanted to hug him, but since I never had before, I felt it might be awkward. Fortunately, Mama and Mrs. Spaulding had spotted us in the kitchen and had decided to join us.

"Hot out there," Mrs. Spaulding announced, dabbing her neck with a paper towel. Surely she could have found something more elegant than that to swab her sweat. Then I remembered the joke. Southern women don't sweat. They glow. So I figured any kind of material would do in that case.

"Mary Alice Spaulding, what are you trying to do?" It was the grating voice familiar to us all. The voice of my grandmother. We had all noticed that Mimi had spent most of the recent days in her room with the window air conditioner turned to stun. You could hang meat in there.

"I'm sorry?" Mrs. Spaulding looked genuinely surprised. We all did.

"Kathleen." Mimi looked at me. "Malcolm." She didn't look at him but just waved her hand in his general direction. "Would you two excuse us please? Chandler, don't you have something to paint?" Rage welled up in me, the kind I had felt earlier in the summer, the kind that had made me run away and made me want to stay away forever.

My grandmother's tone was condescending. I looked at my mother, expecting her to retaliate. I could see an unfamiliar anger on her face. But before she could open her mouth, Mrs. Spaulding jumped in.

"Kathleen, Malcolm, honey. Can you excuse us please? I'm afraid this is just adult talk you wouldn't be interested in." Then Mrs. Spaulding looked at my mother. "Chan, you don't have to..."

The fire in my mother's eyes subsided. "It's okay, Mary Alice. I'll be working on the porch if you need me."

My mother gave me a reassuring nod. She could tell, I think, how outraged I was and that impudent words were just dying to spill out of my mouth. After a return nod to my mother, Malcolm and I dutifully walked off together. But instead of going back to my room, I walked behind Malcolm into his. He turned around to close the door and was just as surprised to see me as I was at being there.

"Kath-a-leen. You can come in if you want to," he said.

I didn't dare sit on the bed. That was his. His sickbed. I spotted a small stool in the corner that I hadn't noticed before, and I sat on that.

"Nice room," I said hoping he didn't know I had invaded his space a few times in his absence.

"Yeah, it's my room." He proudly put his hand on his chest.

I thought, beneath that hand beats a very weak heart. I almost cried.

We had left the door to Malcolm's room slightly opened. I glanced out into the main room and saw Mrs. Spaulding and my grandmother still standing there, silently looking at each other. They looked like those fake wrestlers on TV, squaring off, each circling the other, perusing, waiting for the right moment to pounce. My grandmother held out a long, thin piece of paper. A check, maybe. I moved the stool I was sitting on closer to the door.

Malcolm looked at me as if to scold me. "Kath-a-leen." It was a gentle warning, and I did not heed it.

"Malcolm, there's something going on around here, and I want to find out what it is."

He cocked his head and looked at me intently. He seemed at a loss for words.

The women moved into a far corner of the kitchen, out of my line of sight. The conversation was spirited, but I could hear only bits and pieces of it. Every time one of the women would raise her voice, it would prompt the other to lower hers on the retort.

I did hear this. Plain and clear.

"Mary Alice Jenkins, ever since college you've been one-upping me. You were Sigma Chi sweetheart, and I never was more than a little sister. You were homecoming queen, and I was just an attendant."

I almost laughed out loud. My grandmother, who had switched to using her old friend's maiden name, was raising the most ridiculously petty argument I had ever heard. It sounded like something I might hear on the grammar school playground.

"Margaret, honey. That was a hundred years ago. Let's keep our differences current, shall we?" I noted a rare bit of condescension in Mrs. Spaulding's tone.

"Fine." And then the volume decreased once again. I stood up, unashamedly eavesdropping.

I hoped neither my father nor Dorothy would enter the room and interrupt. This was getting good.

The differences between the two were not just current. In the following moments of the conversation, I learned a lot more than I had known about my history and my family's journey with the Spauldings.

Although I had already sensed and confirmed my illegitimate conception, I still felt a considerable amount of information had been left out.

TRUE: my mother had been pregnant with me when my parents married. TRUE: my parents had moved back to Jackson and had lived under the thumb of the Morton millions. TRUE: my mother had never been accepted as one of the family. I noted again: my mother had been different. Artsy. Flighty. Beautiful. I truly believed she was beautiful, and though I had been enraged at her lately, even thought I loathed her a few weeks before, I still knew that both inside and out she was a beautiful person. She had put up with unkind treatment from my grandparents, and had dealt with it the only way she knew how—by getting away from the environment under the guise of furthering her art. However, her creativity had not suffered. Maybe it had flourished as she had learned to express herself so gloriously on canvas or on paper.

I didn't learn all the facts that day, though I heard enough to stun me and make the colored lines of my life bleed together for the first time. Some of it I learned much later, and I eventually pieced it together with inferences in the conversation.

Chapter Thirty-three

Mary Alice Jenkins had married Walter Spaulding, a handsome gentleman from the Louisiana bayou who had come to the University of Alabama on an academic scholarship, the only way he could have attended any college because his family was dirt poor. I wondered why the women even brought it up. I guessed they were covering old ground to get to the newest rift between them.

Margaret Ann Boswell (my grandmother), had seen the good-looking, intelligent Walter first. She had met him at a mixer on the quad, and Margaret had flirted with him unashamedly. I didn't even want to imagine that. Her mistake, she said, was introducing Walter to her friend, Mary Alice. Apparently there had been no immediate sparks between Walter and Mary Alice, and Margaret had pursued Mr. Spaulding without restraint. That was, until she found out his financial status, or lack of it, Mary Alice added.

Mary Alice, however, had found Mr. Spaulding to be kind and gentle and a wonderful man indeed. He began to pursue her, and she married him after they both graduated from college. The next summer, Walter drilled for and found oil, lots of oil, on his family's property in Louisiana. Being the sharp businessman that he was, within five years Walter Spaulding had turned the boom into millions plus.

Margaret, having already married Everett Morton, the rich (but even I knew brash) frat boy from Jackson, had fallen into the easy lap of old money. She, however, believed that hers was not as wonderful as the life the lovely, serene Mary Alice was living. Though Mary Alice tried through the years to communicate with Margaret, obviously my grandmother's jealousy of the Spauldings' success could not be quelled. Margaret admitted right then and there that she'd seethed for twenty years.

The rivalry raised its head again when Mary Alice and Walter hosted a summer rush party in one of their mansions near the Alabama campus. It was there that my father met my mother. The connections went back further than I had imagined. No wonder there was such familiarity around the table.

And that was where I entered the picture. My grandmother held Mrs. Spaulding responsible for bringing my mother (and thus me) into their family. That's what I thought anyway. There was so much more.

"All I did was encourage a gifted artist to continue her pursuits of excellence. Chandler is a brilliant artist, Margaret. You know it as well as I. She could have been world renowned, but she chose to stay in Jackson with George and Kat, and I believe that was the right decision." It brought the daunting remembrance of the legal separation announcement a few weeks back. I would want Mrs. Spaulding to remind my parents of the choices they made and would be responsible in the choices they were to make. "All I did was give your daughter-in-law an outlet for her gift by providing her places to paint and galleries to show her work."

"All you did was throw your money into a pot of guilt, you mean."

I hardly recognized my grandmother's voice, which had taken an almost demonic tone. Perhaps our Mrs. Spaulding had been our benefactor for all those years. Perhaps she had funded my mother's career entirely. I had never asked how we had been supported. I just imagined that the Morton money had sent us to all those colonies. Obviously I had been wrong.

"Margaret…" Mrs. Spaulding seemed to be mustering all the restraint she could. "We sponsored colonies for aspiring artists like Chan all over the country, and Chandler has earned whatever accolades she has gotten."

"You bankrolled her. Kept encouraging her. Kept her seeking out this…this…art dream. Traipsing all over the place dragging my granddaughter with her." For once I almost agreed with Mimi; I would have at the beginning of this agonizing summer.

Mary Alice Spaulding went silent. Since I couldn't see her, I didn't know if she had left the room or was just pausing to let the dust settle.

Finally she spoke. "Margaret Ann, we both have been so blessed. We've each had so much money we couldn't spend it all. Lord knows we've tried though, huh?" Her lame attempt at adding levity to the heated moment met silence.

"You always had more," my grandmother said. She sounded tired and spent. "I don't begrudge you so much for that. I just hate you for try-ing to buy my family and now trying to buy a story in the newspaper about how a kind-hearted millionairess saves the life of a sick retarded child." She drew a billboard or marquee in the air with her hands.

That was it. The check. I was getting good at this. Apparently Mrs. Spaulding had written a check to cover the cost of Malcolm's surgery. I guessed my grandmother was angry because she hadn't thought of it first. She had lent her cook and her own presence at this place in hopes that it would be enough to purchase a morsel of admiration. But Mary Alice Spaulding had one-upped her again. A chill went over me to think how petty adults can be, and my stomach turned sour when I realized the adult in question was my grandmother.

The conversation died, fading as if each contestant was just waiting for the other to deal the fatal blow. I turned to see what Malcolm thought of the situation, but he was fast asleep on his bed. Perhaps he had missed the whole thing.

Chapter Thirty-four

Malcolm came to the breakfast table looking a little stronger than he had the day before.

"I'm hungry, y'all," he announced to the delight of his guardian and the rest of us.

"Oh, glory!" Jeanette exclaimed. "Malcolm, why don't you return thanks?"

The saying of the blessing at every meal was something I had gotten used to. Mama would bow her head out of respect to her hosts, but she never closed her eyes. I know because I never closed my eyes either. We didn't, however, look around disrespectfully. We both just kept our gaze on the center of our plates and waited until the *amen*. Usually Jeanette would lead the prayer. Most of the time it was short and sweet. "Heavenly Father, make us thankful for these and all the many blessings you've give us" often preceded an added special request or thanks that was currently on her mind.

Malcolm intertwined his left hand fingers with his right and closed his eyes super tight. The others at the table took their usual postures. My mother and I were open-eyed but reverent. Jeanette was open-handed with her eyes closed and her palms up to the sky. My father folded his hands in his lap and closed his eyes, as did his mother, though the bitterness in my grandmother was evident even in her bowed posture. Mrs. Spaulding bowed her head and closed her eyes.

Malcolm took a deep breath and then coughed a little. "Oh Lord. Thank you for this food and for my friends and for my family. Help me have a good operation. Amen."

As he spoke, Mrs. Spaulding's lips formed a silent version of his words.

My father had been out deep-sea fishing the day before, and his face, except for his upper forehead, had gotten severely burned. So had his forearms.

Mrs. Spaulding recommended Noxzema to take out the sting. Mimi suggested butter. Jeanette offered to apply compresses of vinegar and baking soda. But my mother gently wrapped his forearms in towels drenched with cold water and turned them over or replaced them when their effectiveness wore off. It seemed to relieve his pain although the redness remained.

I was blissful. The tenderness my mother was showing my father was a sure sign that they were still together. I just knew that any minute they would tell me the official separation was off and the marriage was going to be rebuilt. I was already having visions of family harmony I had never even imagined before.

The rancor in my grandmother, however, magnified. She began taking her meals in her room. I wondered how long she would stay around. And if she left, would she take Dorothy with her?

The newest issue of *Tiger Beat* had just hit the newsstands, and I asked permission to walk down to Alvin's to get it.

"Can I walk with you?" my mother asked. I hadn't planned on that. In fact, I had hoped to lengthen my absence just a bit and drop in on Barry and the Hangout.

"Uh, sure," I said.

"Haven't been school shopping yet," Mama said as we walked the two hundred or so yards down the highway to the store.

"I don't think Alvin's is the place for school clothes," I said.

"No, I wasn't thinking that. On our way home next week, I guess we need to veer either over to Mobile or up to Montgomery and find you some clothes. I'll bet you've outgrown everything…"

"Stop!" I was not willing to go on without full disclosure of her intentions. "I'm not a child, Mama. You can tell me what's going on. Daddy told me we were going back to Jackson, but that's all he'd say. What is going on with you? I can't keep on guessing, Mother." I hoped the formal address would get an honest response.

"Okay." My mother herded me over onto the beach side of the highway. We trekked through a field of sea oats for a few steps and sat on a dune that looked like it hadn't ever been walked on before. I was thankful for the cloud cover that kept the sun from baking us. In the oppressive humidity, I made a silent vow not to leave that place until somebody told me what was happening.

"Kat, you're right. You're not a child, and so we, your dad and I, figure it's time to be honest with you."

Now I was going to hear the truth. Or maybe just my mother's version of it.

"I'm listening."

My mother threaded a reed from the sea oats between her fingers. She twisted it into a shape that looked like a dove. My mother was so gifted that even her mindless doodling was a masterpiece.

"I guess you've learned a lot this summer about things," she began. "You learned how your dad and I got married, how we came back to Jackson…"

I interrupted, hoping to hasten the conclusion, since there was a thundercloud moving toward us. "How we made all those trips to artist colonies."

"You heard the conversation between Mary Alice and your—"

"Yes. I heard." My body started to tremble and my stomach churned. I tried to suppress my anger.

Mama continued. "Kat, I'm not trying to excuse anything, but the last thirteen years have been…tough. Not the part that included you."

"Mama, wait. Don't apologize. I know you love me. I know Daddy loves me."

"We do, Kat. We do. I promise you that." She grabbed my arm and pleaded for me to believe her. I did. And I hoped I wouldn't cry.

I looked into her pained eyes and was afraid of what her response would be. "But I want more than anything for you and Daddy to love each other."

Mama withdrew and sat silent for a few seconds. "I can't promise that will happen," she said with a hint of finality.

I started to cry just as the rain began to fall. Though I was grateful my parents were apparently willing to stay married for my sake or for some other sake, I didn't want either of them to live in a "prison," as my mother had called it. I wanted them to love each other and live together happily. That fantasy, if I understood my mother's statement, was never going to be real.

Chapter Thirty-five

Wednesday was wash day at the cabin, but that particular Wednesday included packing for Malcolm and Jeanette. Mrs. Spaulding would be going along, too, driving all three of them to Ochsner's Clinic in New Orleans the next day. Mrs. Spaulding had been living out of a suitcase anyway for several days, and all she had to do was wash out a few things and pack them back into her leather suitcase. There was a sense of both excitement and foreboding, though no one expressed it verbally.

The weather over the past twenty-four hours had been temperamental. It wasn't uncommon for summer thundershowers to move in and out quickly, but these storms were violent and packed with rain and wind and explosive lightning.

Weather frightened Jeanette. She wouldn't use the telephone during a storm, nor let anyone else use it. The TV and radio were unplugged, all windows and doors were closed and locked, and she would try to huddle us all into the center of the cabin, which we often would respectfully ignore, until the lightning passed. There had been times even I had been a little unnerved by the electrical bolts from the sky and the sound they carried, but I never wanted to let on.

"Put on your tennises, Kath-a-leen." Malcolm pointed to my feet once during a spectacular lightning storm.

"My what?" I asked.

"Your tennises, shoes with rubber soles. Jeanette says"—he shook his finger in a perfect imitation of her—"Rubber won't let 'lectricity pass through your body like regular soles." I rolled my eyes at another one of Jeanette's old wives' tales. It was like turning your hat around or cussing a black cat walking across your path.

I put on my tennis shoes to appease Malcolm, but I still refused to turn my hat around in the presence of a black cat.

The clouds over the gulf growled all morning like a hungry stomach.

Daddy announced at lunch, "Weatherman says the satellites picked up a tropical depression way out at sea." I couldn't imagine how that would affect me. "Could develop into a hurricane and be coming this way." I had never experienced a hurricane. There had been some storms that had come up through the gulf and had hit Mobile before, but Jackson was far enough inland that we hardly ever got more than heavy rain.

"Oh, Lord," Jeanette interjected. I could see she was already tensing up. I was a little disappointed that a woman of apparent dynamic faith would have such a fear of nature. "The power of the hand o' God is sumpin' I don't wanna mess with" was her explanation. I took it to mean she trusted God but didn't want to challenge His power. So she put on her rubber-soled shoes and unplugged appliances during every thunderstorm just to be sure.

It took about half an hour for the relatively mild storm to unleash all its power. Shortly after that, the sun came out, and the steam that rose off the asphalt highway was so dense that it almost obstructed our view of the bay on the other side.

My days at this place were winding down. I had already expressed to "Dear Diary" my mixed emotions about leaving. Though I had resisted admitting it, this was a beautiful place. When I finally forced myself to look at the pure white sand, the sparkling shoreline, and the grace of the waterfowl that flew overhead and landed on the beach, I was struck as Mama was at the wonder of nature. I agreed this had been indeed an ingenuous design.

"You going swimming, Kath-a-leen?" Malcolm walked past me carrying an armload of clean and folded clothes.

Since I was wearing my swimsuit and carrying a beach towel, I thought it was fairly obvious, but I didn't bark at him. "Yeah, thought I would."

Storms out at sea often brought seaweed to the shore. The brown wiry masses of vegetation would churn in the surf and sometimes play host to tiny sea creatures. Several times Malcolm had shown me small shrimp he had found in the seaweed. I hadn't been too impressed with his discoveries at first, but after a while, I realized he was fascinated by seemingly unimportant but fabulous details in nature.

I walked toward the surf and studied the shoreline. I didn't see much seaweed in the water. I knew that the seaweed wouldn't hurt me, but it was a little unnerving to have it brush against my leg in the surf.

The waves were high and they looked inviting. It didn't take me long to wade up to my shins in it, but I wouldn't stay there. The force was so strong that it could knock my feet out from under me even at that depth. I knew that would draw me down into the sandy bottom and get grit in my bathing suit. I waded a little farther. Waist high was perfect. I could jump and dip with the waves, even use my body as a surfboard and ride them to the shore if I wanted.

Sunbathers and swimmers started to dot the beach. The afternoon sun looked like it was there to stay. The water was crystal clear and soothing. I reached a sandbar farther out, and the waves lapped around my knees. As I waded away from the shore, the water got darker. There were sandbars all over the gulf floor, and past them were deep pools where I couldn't even touch bottom. However, there had always been another sandbar just beyond that I would swim to and marvel at the fact that I could stand up with most of my body out of the water so far from the edge.

That day, that surf was different. At the first sandbar, the current was strong enough to pull my feet out from under me. Even in the shallower water, it was hard for me to stand up. I tried to swim parallel to the shoreline, but the harder I swam, the farther I drifted from my point of entry. I was struggling to keep my head out of water. I had been told about undertow, a force of undercurrent in the gulf that was very dangerous and must be respected. I had noticed red flags flying down at Long Beach when the undertow was supposed to be strong. Swimmers were not allowed on public beaches where lifeguards worked to enter the surf and were highly cautioned when the flag flew yellow. I was sure at that moment Barry was flying a red flag at his beach. If I had known the struggle I was about to face, I would have never entered the water at all.

I wouldn't panic. I had been warned not to. It was the first rule in water safety, especially in water as unpredictable as the gulf. Instead of struggling against the pull of the current I decided to ride it, floating and paddling down the shoreline. However, the current was taking me out further away from the beach.

The other swimmers I had seen were keeping themselves close to the shore, and I couldn't even venture a guess as to how far away from them I was, nor how far I had drifted from my original entry point. I couldn't see our cabin from where I was, and I had to remind myself again not to panic.

I had the urge to call for help, and I figured I should do it before I lost my strength. No one could possibly hear me. The roar of the surf was loud enough that my voice wouldn't reach those along the edge. Occasionally I would see a swimmer look my way. I tried to wave and call out several times. A few of the swimmers waved back, apparently not realizing I was in trouble. Still I tried to remain calm. I was a strong swimmer and could tread water a long time if I kept steadily breathing and moving my arms and legs enough to keep my head above water. Suddenly I felt a calm come over me, but immediately after the calm came a realization that it might be a sign that I was giving up. I was no longer struggling to survive. I was letting this force sweep me away, and I mustered a new resolve to fight it. In fact, I tried to merge all the strong feelings I had had in the past months, hoping they would combine into a burst of energy that would get me out of trouble.

For some reason, Malcolm's face came to my mind; not just the face he showed me every day, but his face of unswerving faith after the day I'd asked him if he was afraid of the surgery.

"No. Not at all. God will take care of me," he'd said.

I wished for that kind of faith. Looking toward the shore once more, I saw Malcolm. I so hoped this wasn't a hallucination. I couldn't for the life of me figure out how Malcolm could be so far down the beach at the exact point I was bobbing in the gulf water.

"Help!" I waved, hoping he wouldn't think I was just greeting him. He waved back, but not a playful wave. He was yelling something, too. I convinced myself this was not a vision my mind was hoping to see, but that Malcolm actually was running down the beach following my bobbing body. After each yell, I could see him stop to catch his breath and sometimes to cough. I knew Malcolm would go for help. I just hoped I could hang on long enough for him to do so.

Then he entered the water.

"Go back, Malcolm. Go back!" I screamed. Surely he was not going to try to rescue me. Malcolm was an average swimmer at best. If he tried to come after me, he too would get caught in this current. Only a trained lifeguard would know what to do. Like Barry and his friend, who had rescued a child with one of them as an anchor on the beach while the other swam out into the water. But I was drifting in the opposite direction from Long Beach, and with every bob I made in the surf, Barry and his lifeguard partner were getting farther and farther away.

Malcolm looked up and down the shore. He entered the water again. "No! No! Malcolm, don't! Get help!"

Suddenly he broke into a sprint down the beach, in the direction I was drifting. A full sprint for Malcolm was hardly a casual jog for someone else. Malcolm's lack of muscle tone limited his ability to run very fast at all. I had seen him running once as fast as he could to catch something interesting he'd seen washed up on the beach before the tide carried it back out again. It had only been a black rubber flipper that someone had lost while snorkeling or had accidentally left too near the surf. I wondered where Malcolm was running to. I wondered if he could find help in time.

He disappeared between the dunes and the buildings for a moment. He returned alone, apparently unable to find a rescuer. Malcolm frantically waved at me again and shouted something I could not hear. Then he coughed deeply, bent over, and rested his hands on his knees. I wondered if both of us would die that day.

I wasn't moving fast, but I was moving steadily. Always, when I looked at the shore, Malcolm was right with me. No telling how many miles we were away from home.

My legs were cramping, so I stretched out parallel with the surface of the gulf, hoping the saltwater would buoy my body while I relaxed my muscles for a bit. I was starting to get sleepy, too. I tried lying on my back and closing my eyes. Every few seconds, my head would go under the water, and I would snap back to reality. I tried to think of something pleasant. I couldn't think of anything. It didn't matter. I needed to do something that would not lull me into the grips of the deep.

Sing. I would sing to keep my mind alert and my voice strong. Two verses and choruses of "Chain of Fools" was enough to carry me another fifty yards. I tried to remember all the words to "Aquarius," and the mental gymnastics helped me focus so I could survive another minute.

"I've got peace like a river. I've got peace like a river. I've got peace like a river in my soul." It was the only other song I could think of. I quickly deemed it too sedate, however, and therefore more dangerous to my situation. I sang it anyway until I could think of another one. I tried to get a picture of Baltimore Rachel and Paul in my head. I imagined Paul with his guitar and Rachel with her Bible talking about me, figuring I was a runaway and deciding whether they should turn me into the police. That thought caused the rage to well up in me, and every muscle seemed to tighten. That was good. Anger would help me continue to struggle. It would help me survive.

The water lapped over my face once, then again. Something I had read in the Bible stood out in my mind. "I vowed to look for new mercies, but I never found them." As the truth of that verse chilled me, Malcolm faded from my view.

Chapter Thirty-six

Y ou're in the hospital, honey. You're safe. Wake up."

I didn't want to wake up. My whole body ached. I felt like I had a lead weight on my chest, and I just wanted to rest until it went away.

A white-uniformed nurse stood out against the other people I recognized. I wanted to ask where I was and what had happened, but the pain in my throat was excruciating. I tried to speak, but nothing would come out.

Someone said, "The saltwater irritated her throat and lungs. It'll get better with time." I wanted to say, "I'm right here. I can hear you." But I couldn't gather the strength to respond.

I closed my eyes again, hoping to rest, but a horrible thought rushed through my mind.

My eyes popped open and I opened my mouth. With the last morsel of strength I thought I had, I whispered, "Malcolm?"

"He's right here, honey." I was glad to recognize my mother's voice and elated to see Malcolm step closer to the bed.

"Oh boy," he mouthed. Then he turned away and coughed.

For a few minutes I tried to put it all together. I had been drowning in the gulf and somehow Malcolm had rescued me. I couldn't believe we had both survived. I began to say a prayer of thanks, but I was too tired to finish it, and I let the weariness pull me into sleep.

I woke up and it was dark outside the window. Raising my head to look around the room, I realized my mother was the only one who remained.

"Where is everybody?" My voice was thin and parched.

My mother sprang to her feet and was holding my hand in an instant.

"There you are." Mama smiled down at me. She had her hair up in a knot on top of her head, which made her bronze neck look even longer and more graceful than usual. I wondered how long I had been there and how long I had been adrift in the gulf.

"Mama? Where is everybody?"

"You just rest. Okay? Doctor says you're going to be just fine. You scared us to death, Kathleen."

"No, where is everybody?"

My mother didn't answer. Instead she reached across my body and pushed a button on the end of a cord that lay on the bed beside me.

"Yes?" A voice came out of nowhere.

"My daughter is awake. Can you send in a nurse?"

"Of course."

A few minutes later, a nurse put a thermometer in my mouth, held two fingers against my wrist, and looked at her watch. She wrote something on a piece of paper attached to a clipboard. Next she pumped up the cuff around my upper arm, put her stethoscope to her ears, and listened to something in my arm while she released the air in the cuff. She wrote something else on the paper. I realized my mother was no longer in the room. Perhaps she had stepped into the bathroom. Thinking of bathroom, I had the sudden urge to go.

"Take it easy, honey. Don't get up too soon. I'll help you if you need to get up."

"My mother will help me." I didn't want a perfect stranger, even if she was a nurse, helping me with bathroom activities.

"I think your mother stepped down the hall for a second. Want me to call her?" The nurse's face came into focus. She was older, a few gray hairs peeking out from under her stiff white hat, but with a pleasant smile.

I nodded.

The nurse left, but my mother did not return. I wondered why. I wondered where my father was. I had seen him in the gathering of people around my bed before. Or had I? Where was Malcolm? Where was everybody? Panic tried to wash over me again, and I told myself to relax and breathe deeply as I had in the gulf just a short time ago. But my lungs were heavy and when I tried to fill them with air, it was like they had ignited. My insides were on fire, and I was totally alone.

Chapter Thirty-seven

They had officially named the tropical storm Camille by the time I was released from the hospital. But I didn't care about the storm, its path, or its possible wrath. I was more concerned about what had happened to Malcolm.

My mother told me he had collapsed outside my hospital room. Fortunately, one of the doctors on call had been Malcolm's regular doctor, the one who had been the connection to Ochsner's Clinic. He decided Malcolm shouldn't make the trip to New Orleans in his weakened condition. Apparently, Malcolm had actually had a heart attack.

I didn't want to go home or back to the cabin. I wanted to stay at the hospital and wait for Malcolm to recover. Someone had brought me clean clothes, and I was ready to stay as long as it took for him to get well.

"How can this happen?" I pleaded, still weak from my near-death experience. "He's sixteen. Only old people have heart attacks."

My mother explained to me that Malcolm's exertions the day he saved me had put extra stress on his heart, with its deformed valve.

"It's my fault," I cried. "He was trying to save me."

I was told that while I was drifting dangerously in the gulf, Malcolm had gone to the nearest cabin and had told someone there to call for help. He had remembered the phone number at our cabin and had told someone to call there, too. When he returned to the shore, he had seen me struggling and going under the water. He had not wanted to wait for a rescue team, so he decided to plunge into the water himself. As I would have guessed, he too got caught in the strong undertow and was dragged out to sea with me. Help had arrived just before we sank for the last time. Rescuers had pulled us both out. There was still the question in my mind of why Malcolm had been on the shore to begin with.

"Even if we do think moving him is worth the risk, that tropical storm has turned into a hurricane, and the roads between here and New Orleans are likely to close anytime," I overheard the doctors tell the band of vigil keepers, which included me, my mother and father, Jeanette, and Mary Alice. Dorothy and my grandmother had stayed back at the cabin for some reason.

"Can that doctor come here to Panama City?" Mrs. Spaulding asked. "Seems like that would be the safest thing right now. If it's money he needs…"

The doctor interrupted, "Even if the surgeon came here, we don't have the equipment he would need to do the operation. Besides, I'm not sure Malcolm could withstand the surgery now anyway."

Jeanette sat silent in the corner of the waiting room, staring out the window. I wasn't sure she had heard what the doctor said or not. She appeared to be in such despair that she didn't act connected to the rest of us at all.

Malcolm had been put in the intensive care unit and could only have visitors a few minutes a day. That was the only reason Jeanette couldn't keep constant watch over him.

I tried to imagine what might be going on in her mind. Was she blaming me like I was blaming myself?

On impulse I went to her and put my hand on her shoulder. I realized it was the first time I had ever touched the lady. She looked at me and suddenly I feared her wrath. I could remember her many diatribes directed toward the soap opera actors on TV. I expected her to unleash on me as she had on Lisa of "As the World Turns." I was ready for her wrath to explode on me. I deserved it. Instead, she reached out and touched my hand and said, "He's in the Lord's hands, hon. He's in the Lord's hands."

Before an hour passed, the waiting room had filled up with people I had never seen. Old people, young people, and children came to bring prayers, tears, and food. My mother and Mrs. Spaulding took over the greeting and the taking of food dishes while Jeanette spent her time talking and praying with small groups of people. I learned after a while that these were members of the church that she and Malcolm attended regularly.

"I'm still not sure why people bring food in cases like this. There's a perfectly good cafeteria right down the hall," my mother commented after taking a tiny slice of a lemon pound cake someone had brought.

"It's the Southern way, Chandler. We figure food will cure every sorrow," Mrs. Spaulding explained.

Sorrow? Malcolm wasn't gone. He was still alive, and so sorrow was not appropriate. Hope was what we needed, I resolved. I closed my eyes for a few seconds and said a prayer, the first I ever remember praying.

"God, don't let Malcolm die. Amen."

My father left the waiting room and walked down the hall. I followed him and saw he was going to the pay phone. I held back and leaned against the wall, hoping he wouldn't think I was eavesdropping. I wasn't really; I was looking for an opportunity to get my father alone so we could talk. I could tell it was my grandmother on the other end of the telephone line because I heard him ask, "When's Dad getting here?" I hoped that was why Mimi and Dorothy had not come to the hospital, that they had been awaiting Papa's arrival and would accompany him to the hospital later.

"Papa's coming?" I asked Daddy after he hung up the phone.

"Uh yeah. He is. He's on his way."

Daddy put his arm around my waist. I had grown taller over the summer, and it looked like it surprised him that he didn't have to reach down to hug me anymore.

"Daddy, do you think Malcolm's gonna be all right?"

My father sighed and shook his head. "I don't know, Bee-bee. The doctors say he's pretty sick right now."

Hearing that made me start to cry. I had been waiting for someone to say something, to predict what might occur. This was the first time I had heard anyone venture a guess. I covered my face with my hands as if that would make this scene go away.

"Daddy, he can't die. He just can't." I turned and wept into his shoulder. My father placed his arms gently around me and let me keep on weeping. He was silent as though he, too, were heartbroken.

There were too many people in the main waiting room, so Daddy and I took the elevator down a floor and found another room with a TV. All the channels were covering the hurricane, and reporters were saying everybody along the Gulf Coast needed to be on alert.

"Does that mean us?" I asked.

"Yeah, it does. Earlier the reports said the hurricane was still out about a hundred miles, but it had stalled."

"That's good, isn't it?"

"Not really. It could pick up more strength out in the gulf. And it could come inland anywhere. Hurricanes are notoriously unpredictable."

I wanted to ask if we were in danger. I wanted to ask again if Malcolm was going to make it. I wanted to ask a lot of things, but instead I said another silent prayer. "God, don't let the hurricane hit us. Amen."

Papa Morton arrived with an entourage. His driver and his assistant, who were almost always in tow, were accompanied this time by my grandmother and Dorothy.

"Son!" My grandfather stood at the end of the hall of the hospital, looking like the millionaire he was. Pinstriped suit, Italian leather shoes, silk tie, and monogrammed shirt. His powder-white hair was slicked back, and he smoothed it with his diamond-studded hand.

"Hey, Dad." My father walked to greet him. An obligatory hug was exchanged. Next to my grandfather, my dad looked like a bum. None of us had slept in several hours, and my father hadn't shaved in as long.

"Boy, you look terrible," my grandfather barked. My grandmother, who looked like she'd just had her hair done at a salon, nodded in agreement. The driver and the assistant stood two paces behind my grandparents. Dorothy was three more paces behind them.

Daddy managed a smile. "Thanks, Dad. You, too."

My grandmother chimed in. "We've packed all your things, Georgie, and it's time to get out of here."

"Excuse me?" I stepped out from behind my father. My grandfather didn't even look at me. With my drastic hair change and my growth spurt, I was pretty sure he didn't recognize me.

"Kathleen, the storm's headed this way. If we hurry, we can make it home and batten down our hatches," Mimi added.

"Mimi, Jackson is over two hundred miles from here. The storm won't hit there. It's too far inland." I looked at my father for verification, because I really had no idea what I was talking about. He nodded.

"Nonsense," barked my grandfather. "We've packed your things, and you're going home with us." He hadn't packed a thing. That was why he'd brought his assistant and his driver. These two and Dorothy had done the packing, and my grandmother had gone out to have her hair done. My grandfather had probably made a visit to one of the many liquor stores he owned while the others did all the work.

"You can leave my things here. I'm not going." I turned and ran back down the hall.

My mother met me outside the waiting room. "What's wrong, Kat?"

I pointed to the end of the hall. My mother raised an eyebrow and started toward the group of people standing there. "Everett, what's going on?"

I eased back down the hall to see how my mother was going to address her in-laws.

"I've come to take us all home," my grandfather answered as though he were Mighty Mouse and had come to save the day.

"You've what?" My mother looked at my father. Daddy's gaze was affixed to the shiny linoleum floor.

My grandfather turned on his imported heels and headed for the elevator. "We'll be leaving in"—he looked at his Rolex watch—"ten minutes."

His Parade of Obedience peeled off behind him. As the elevator opened, only Dorothy looked back at us. She seemed surprised that we returned her look of disbelief.

"I'm not going," I reiterated. "Tell them to leave my stuff down in the lobby or something, but I'm not leaving."

"George?" My mother folded her arms and stared at her husband, who still had not looked up at her.

My father reached out and put his hand on the nape of my neck. Slowly, he raised his head until his eyes met mine. "I love you, honey. I love you so much." And then he turned and walked slowly away down the empty hallway and into the elevator.

My mother stared blankly at the elevator for a second and then seemed to remember I was still standing next to her. She shook her head and said, "I'm sorry."

"Sorry for what? Are you going, too?" I raised my voice and then noticed a stern look on the face of a nurse sitting behind a desk. "Are you going back with them?"

Mama's eye widened with surprise. "No!" The nurse shushed her. My mother held up her hand in an apology to the woman. "I'm sorry you have to go through all this. You're so young." Mama's voice broke off, and her eyes filled up with tears.

I was beginning to understand at least one thing. My mother wasn't apologizing for my family's conflicts; she was apologizing because I had learned of them in such an inflammatory environment.

"Mama, you do what you want to. You go home if you like. I'm staying here with Malcolm. He stayed with me on that beach, and I won't leave him now." I walked past my mother and opened the door to the waiting room to summon Mrs. Spaulding.

"Everett was here?" Mrs. Spaulding asked after I relayed to her the events of the past few moments.

"He still is, I think. He said he would wait ten minutes."

The same apologetic look that my mother had had came over Mrs. Spaulding's face. I knew they were both sorry I had found out so many disturbing things in such a short amount of time. My mother was still standing where I had left her. She had wrapped her arms around herself because no one else was there to do it for her.

"Chan." Mrs. Spaulding's chin quivered, and then her eyes got moist. She went to my mother. "I don't know what to say." Mama's arms didn't unfold. Mrs. Spaulding's just folded over them, and I wrapped mine around them both.

Chapter Thirty-eight

Two suitcases and three boxes I recognized as belonging to Mama and me were stacked in the corner of the empty hospital lobby. There was no sign of my grandfather's entourage anywhere. It was twenty minutes past the ten-minute limit, but I had ridden the elevator down just to see. Except for a nice older lady wearing a pink-and-white striped uniform sitting behind a desk, there was no one in sight. I scanned the parking lot. No Cadillacs with Alabama plates remained. My grandparents and my father were gone.

The candy striper looked up and smiled as I walked past her dragging a large suitcase behind me.

"That's a heavy load for a little thing like you," she observed. I knew she meant well, but I did not like to be referred to as "a little thing." I pushed the suitcase into the open elevator door. I would have to make several trips to gather all of our belongings.

Mary Alice Spaulding and my mother were still standing in the hospital hallway talking quietly when the elevator door opened. I pulled at the suitcase and tried to lift it with one arm. I could barely get it off the floor, and so I kept dragging it behind me until the two women looked up and saw me.

"Honey, just leave all that stuff down there." My mother rushed to my aid. Even she couldn't lift the bag, and so she assisted me in dragging it. She didn't ask me if I had seen my father anywhere. It was as if she knew he had gone. I read sad resolve in her face.

Mrs. Spaulding said, "Kathleen, I think I'm going to go back to the cabin while I still can and make sure all the shutters are closed and that it's as secured as it can be. The weather reports still say they don't know exactly where it's going to make landfall. It's just wobbling out there in the gulf. Some people are evacuating already, but I don't think they've closed Highway 98 yet." I nodded.

Mama turned and went back into the waiting room, still without unfolding her arms.

After my mother disappeared behind the waiting room door, I said, "They didn't bring Mama's canvases or her art stuff," a little winded from the load I had been dragging. My lungs were burning some from the saltwater I had inhaled.

"What?" Mrs. Spaulding asked.

"I looked in the boxes. It's just our personal stuff and our clothes. Mama's art stuff must still be on the porch."

"I'll get it all. Don't worry." Mrs. Spaulding patted me on the arm. "I'm sure your grandparents didn't think to close up and bring those things."

I was sure, too, that my grandparents hadn't closed up the cabin, but not because they had forgotten. They wouldn't have done anything out of courtesy for another person, but I appreciated Mrs. Spaulding for not saying what she must believe about my self-absorbed family.

"Mrs. Spaulding," I said as she was fishing the car keys out of her large purse.

"Yes?"

"There's something else they didn't bring. It's just a personal thing of mine."

"Oh? What is it? I'll bring it," she replied after finally locating the keys.

"Well, it's under my bed," I said not wanting to divulge too much.

"Okay. Will I know it...?"

"Just bring it, will you?" I sounded too insolent, and I put my hand over my mouth. "I'm sorry, ma'am. It's personal."

I didn't know what reaction she would have when she found the Bible I had hidden under my bed. I figured she would wonder what I was doing with a Bible with someone else's name on it, but I was also pretty certain she wouldn't ask questions and would bring it to me discreetly.

I went into the waiting room. I had decided not to tell my mother that her art supplies weren't among our meager belongings left in the lobby. I knew she'd thought about it, had even worried just a bit, but she didn't let herself show too much concern.

There were still several people hovering around Jeanette. My mother busied herself with the food table, replacing plastic wrap over cakes, removing used paper plates and cups. I had never felt pity for my mother, ever. But at that moment I could feel nothing else. I was losing my father and my grandparents. She was losing more. Her summer's work could blow away any minute in a violent storm, but worse than that, her life was being swept away, too. Her husband had chosen his heritage over her. And though I felt some of the same pangs of betrayal, it must be more agonizing for her. I was proud that I had defied my grandparents. I was even prouder of my mother for staying with me. At least we would have each other.

The angry words I had used to demean Mama most of that summer were coming back to shame me. Why had I said them? What hurt had I caused her?

The steady stream of visitors to the hospital would change about every half hour or so. It was as if they were tag teams, like wrasslin', as Jeanette called the Saturday night bouts on TV of professional wrestling. I never knew Jeanette and Malcolm had so many friends. But these were from their church, and that's why I had never seen them.

A sweet, older lady came to me with a smile. "You're Kathleen, aren't you?"

"Yes, ma'am."

"Oh yes, you're as precious as Malcolm and Jeanette said you were."

"Ma'am?"

"We all prayed for you when you got lost on the beach that time." I could tell the woman was trying to be gentle, not to remind me of my childish runaway stunt.

"Thank you." That was all I could say.

"We're so thankful you're all right now after getting caught in the undertow. I shudder to think what could have happened. But we're praising the Lord that you're okay."

The woman walked away, but I wanted to shout, "What do you mean you're praising the Lord I'm okay? Malcolm's in intensive care because of me!" But I said nothing. I had to leave the room to keep from breaking into sobs.

I couldn't hold it back. The restroom near the elevator was unoccupied, and I was grateful. I closed and locked the door and turned the handle on the sink. I hoped the sound of water running would drown out my wailing.

"Why? Why? Why?" I looked at my image in the mirror as if it could give me an answer. But I just stared back at my own drawn, pale face and found nothing in it to comfort me.

Chapter Thirty-nine

The storm, still out in the gulf, pushed menacing black clouds overhead that made it impossible to know whether it was day or evening. The clock at the nurses' station said seven. I was pretty sure it was evening because Jeanette had just gone into the ICU, and 7:00 P.M. was one of the designated visiting times. My mother and I watched through the small rectangular windows in the heavy doors. A nurse greeted Jeanette and led her into another room, and Mama and I craned our necks to see if we could catch a glimpse of Malcolm. I almost expected to see him sitting up in the hospital bed with his deep-dimple smile flashing at the sight of his beloved guardian. But the room she entered was dark, and I could see nothing before the door closed behind her.

I looked at Mama, and we moved toward each other at the same time. Intertwining our legs and walking in tandem (like the Monkees did on their TV show) had been a fun game my mother and I had shared long ago. Now that my legs were as long as hers and our strides were the same, it was easier. We walked the length of the hallway without missing a beat.

The waiting room was still running over with visitors. "I know where there's a room that's not so crowded," I said, remembering that my father and I had gone down a floor and found a quiet room with a TV. I didn't tell my mother, that this had been a discovery made by my dad and me. I was sure she didn't want to talk about my father at all, and frankly, neither did I.

The TV reception in the other waiting room looked grainy. I wondered if the storm was starting to affect everything around us. Footage was being shown from the coast of Mississippi. A reporter was standing on a stormy beach near Pascagoula and said that Camille was gaining strength—one-hundred-fifty-mile-per-hour winds—and starting to move again. They were expecting the storm to be the largest hurricane ever to hit the Gulf Coast. It sounded bad.

"How far is Pascagoula from here?" I asked Mama.

"I don't know. I'm not from the South, you know."

Just then a nurse emerged from the hallway. "Wanted to let you all know we're under high alert. Though right now it doesn't look like we're going to be a direct hit, we may be a shelter for those who are evacuating or injured. At this point, management thinks it's better to stay put. If you hear the alarm sound, we'll advise you over the loudspeaker to get to the basement as soon as possible. Okay?"

"Thanks," my mother answered, pulling me close to her.

I sighed.

"What a week," she added. "Let's get back upstairs and see if there's any news on Malcolm."

Jeanette was crying when we intercepted her in the hallway. I feared the worst.

"He looks so sweet lying there," she mumbled among her sobs.

"Any change yet?" Mama asked.

"No, the doctor says there was damage to the heart muscle, but it's hard to tell how bad. He's hopeful that Malcolm's age will be on his side."

Oh, God, let Malcolm's age be on his side.

An hour later, the elevator opened and Mary Alice Spaulding stepped off carrying two large paper sacks. I knew these couldn't contain all of Mama's artwork, but I hoped the Bible had been placed inside one of them. Mrs. Spaulding gave me a reassuring smile.

"Everything is shut up nice and tight at the cabin, Jeanette, so don't worry about a thing. I got some of the stuff out of the refrigerator and brought it with me. Didn't want the electricity to go off and us have a fridge full of spoiled food to deal with." She held up one of the paper sacks. "So, let's eat up." Mrs. Spaulding was trying to sound chipper, I could tell.

Jeanette breathed deeply before she spoke. Still, her voice trembled. "Thank you, Mary Alice. I just saw Malcolm, and he's in a coma but still hanging in there."

"Oh, thank God. Jeanette, thank God." Mrs. Spaulding raised both of her palms to the sky and held them there for a second. Then she remembered. "I brought some basics for you, too. I hope it'll be all right." She held up the other bag. I wasn't sure whether to hope the Bible was in the food bag or in the bag that held Jeanette's underthings. Just as long as I had it, I didn't care how it had gotten there.

"Thank you, hon. I wouldn't mind takin' a shower and puttin' on some fresh clothes. Did you bring my talcum powder?" Jeanette said, digging through the paper bag without waiting for an answer.

I guessed my Bible had been transported in the food bag.

The hospital staff had been so nice to us. They had let us use beds and showers in unoccupied rooms. It apparently had been a light week for patients, but I was afraid that might change when the storm came ashore.

"I'll put this food in that refrigerator they said we could use behind the nurses' station," Mrs. Spaulding said. "I'll be right back."

I wondered if the Hangout was full of teenagers dancing to jukebox music or if it had been deserted because of the approaching storm. I also wondered how the music festival up in New York was going. Since the only TV we had seen was covering Camille's path, I didn't expect to hear how Woodstock went until much later.

Mary Alice Spaulding returned but wasn't carrying the paper bag. I wondered if she had forgotten my Bible. She leaned into me and whispered, "I left it back there in the nurses' lounge." I breathed a slight sigh of relief. "Oh," she added. "Chan, all your work is in the trunk of my car."

Mama and Mrs. Spaulding walked back into the waiting room. The visitor count had thinned out by then to just a couple of people as the day wound down, and I was starting to feel the weight of the past few days. My friend was in a coma because of me, my father and my grandparents had abandoned us, and a storm of historic magnitude might be heading our way. My body ached to sleep but I tried to refocus my mind. While everyone was otherwise occupied, I decided to retrieve my Bible from the nurses' lounge.

"Hello, can I help you?" a nurse asked me as I tried to slip past her.

"Uh, we left some food in the refrigerator."

"Oh yes. Go ahead." She waved me on.

It wasn't that the Bible was so precious to me. It wasn't that I was planning to read it from cover to cover either. I hoped it would be like a good luck charm, or that God would smile on us somehow and pull Malcolm and us through this life-wrenching crisis. I could at least use the distraction of the treasure hunt. I sure needed one.

The paper sack so discreetly placed on the far side of the couch in the lounge contained not at all what I had expected. "What?" I said aloud without meaning to.

Mrs. Beasley smiled weakly at me as I pulled her from the bag. Then it dawned on me. I had put the doll under the bed when I was looking for my diary in the box where she lived. The Bible had gone between the mattress and box springs. I tried to imagine what Mrs. Spaulding's reaction must have been when she pulled Mrs. Beasley from under the bed. She must have thought I needed childhood reassurances, the comfort of an old friend, something like that. It was almost funny until I realized the Bible I had expected to hold in my hand might be lost to the wind and waves. I instinctively caressed Mrs. Beasley and whispered, "God, protect my Bible."

Chapter Forty

n just three months I had learned from Jeannette that letting a chicken fly over your head would cure the chicken pox. I'd learned that letting someone sweep under your feet meant you'd never get married, and that when your nose itched, it was a sign that somebody was coming to visit with a hole in his stocking.

Jeanette Hudspeth was a great puzzle whose pieces, much like mine, seemed never to fit properly. But the more I studied her, the more she made perfect sense. She had minimized her function in life as being the "chief cook and bottle washer" for an artist colony and a lost boy, but I was beginning to hope she would one day realize her grander purpose would include the teaching of self-denial. Her famous fried chicken was an object of that. Frying all of a chicken was the norm in the South. Legs, breasts, thighs, innards—all were cooked and usually eaten. But the worst part of a fryer was what Jeanette called "the last piece that goes over the fence." It was the bony back, which usually included a stub at the end where the tail feathers had once grown. It was this part that Jeanette would eat since no one else would want it. She always said it was her favorite part and pretended to save it back for herself. It was a little thing, and to me at first quite annoying, but it was who Jeanette Hudspeth was. It was who she had taught Malcolm to be.

"He loves you, you know," Jeanette told me at the hospital when there was a lull in the visitor flow.

"Who?" I asked.

"Malcolm. Did you know he asked me once if he could adopt you as his sister?" Jeanette laughed.

"Really?" I was genuinely touched.

"Yeah, but I told 'im it didn't work thataway. That mamas and daddies could adopt chur'n, but that boys couldn't adopt sisters." She laughed again, and I held back tears.

It seemed an appropriate time to ask, "Why was Malcolm out there on the beach the other day when I was drowning? How did he know?"

"Shug, he felt like you needed protectin' from the get-go. He probably followed you more than you know. When you...you know...were gone those three days, he never slept. He stayed up prayin' for you and lookin' for you. He even blamed hisself for lettin' you get away like that." Her voice trailed off. "He'd make a good big brother, I reckon."

To be honest, I had felt Malcolm watching me from time to time. It had greatly irritated me at first. Then it had felt creepy and weird. Then I remember feeling a sense of comfort that somebody was watching over me. I was grateful that Malcolm had taken me under his protection. Otherwise, I would be dead.

I wished the infernal storm would make up its mind, hit us or miss us, so that Malcolm could go on to New Orleans and have his operation. Perhaps waiting on the storm was actually helping Malcolm's heart get stronger, and it had been part of a grand plan after all. I had no one to verify this, but I hoped that if God actually existed, He was putting all of it together for a greater end.

My mother was called to the nurses' station for a long-distance call. I was sure it was my father, but I frankly didn't care what he had to say. His cowardly exit under orders from his pompous father had caused a new leap into understanding for me. The blurred lines about my family were becoming clear. The conversation I had overheard between my grandmother and Mrs. Spaulding, the morsels of truth I had heard from my mother, the whipped-puppy demeanor of my father the day he left us in the hospital were more than enough to sour my affection for him. I would never see him the same again.

"The hurricane looks like it's going to hit west of us. Biloxi and the other towns on the Mississippi coast look like they're going to be hit dead-on," my mother announced after hanging up the phone. I figured my father had been watching the newscasts and had called to let her know that we were in no imminent danger.

I hoped again that it would not be long before we could get Malcolm the medical care he needed.

Mary Alice Spaulding stuck her head in the nurses' lounge where my mother and I were raiding the refrigerator. "He's awake."

Mama and I shoved our food back into the refrigerator and closed the door. We both ran to the ICU door in hopes that it was time for Malcolm to receive visitors. We had waited, what was it, four days?

"I'm sorry." The nurse stopped us before we could enter the hallway. "He's awake but still in intensive care. His mother is the only one allowed in right now."

We knew that Jeanette was not Malcolm's mother, but no one on the medical staff would have guessed that. She and Malcolm shared a last name, and there has never been any mother more loving and attentive than Jeanette.

The remnant of my "family" stood before me. My mother and Mary Alice Spaulding, whom I had known only a few days, were the only people besides Malcolm and Jeanette that I could count on. I was desperately trying to forget I even had a father when my mother announced, "Daddy said to call him collect when you wanted to. I couldn't find you when he called here before." I would not call my father, I vowed, but I nodded to appease my mother.

Two doctors passed us in the hallway and entered the ICU wing. I recognized one of them as having attended to me a few days before. The other I remembered as the doctor who had been Malcolm's primary physician. I hoped their presence on the floor meant something good. Since the two doctors didn't look panicked or even in a hurry when they passed us, I had a feeling they had gotten the word that Malcolm was awake and improving.

"How are you feeling, young lady?" the doctor who had attended me asked a few minutes later as he left the intensive care unit.

"I'm fine. How's Malcolm?" I asked.

"Still a really sick boy, I'm afraid," he answered.

The family doctor joined us. "Jeanette's trying to get him to eat something." He shook his head and smiled. "He's not up to that right now."

"How long will he be in intensive care, doctor?" Mrs. Spaulding asked.

Both of the doctors sighed and looked at each other. One doctor shrugged and the other doctor answered, "There's no way of knowing right now."

My mother asked the question we all wanted to ask: "Will he be able to have the surgery?"

Again the doctors looked unsure. "No way of knowing that either. We've just got to keep him stable and see if we can get past this crisis," one of them answered. "Years of living with the faulty valve have done some damage. The heart attack was not a surprise, actually, but we wanted to get him to Ochsner's before any more damage happened. Then the heart might have had a chance to strengthen on its own." Then he tentatively looked at Mama and me, then back at Jeanette. She seemed to know what he was thinking.

"Oh, it's okay, Doctor. They're family."

Chapter Forty-one

F alling asleep wasn't hard. Staying asleep was. Almost as soon as my eyes would close, the waves would start rolling over me. I could feel the cool water surrounding my body, I could taste the salt in my mouth, and my heart pounded with the same panic I had experienced as I drifted away from safety. The end was always the same. Malcolm's face would appear out of nowhere just before I woke up in a cold sweat.

According to the clock, I had been asleep two hours this time, and it was as dark outside as when I had lain down.

The table next to the hospital bed I had commandeered had three things in the drawer: a small box of tissues, a plastic kidney-shaped tray, and a Bible with the name Gideon engraved on the cover. It was smaller than the one I had been given, and it had no handmade markings at all inside it. It was just pages and pages of words I wouldn't understand even if I knew where to look. I opened the Book randomly anyway and tried to focus my eyes on the first words I came to:

"Save me, O God; for the waters are come in unto my soul."

It was the first thing written under the heading Psalm 69. It seemed to be a little too appropriate to be random since these words could have been my own cry a few days before. I kept reading.

"I sink in deep mire, where there is no standing: I am come into deep waters, where the floods overflow me. I am weary of my crying: my throat is dried: mine eyes fail while I wait for my God."

I hadn't ever thought about waiting for God. In fact, I hadn't really thought about God much at all.

"Hear me, O Lord; for thy lovingkindness is good: turn unto me according to the multitude of thy tender mercies."

There they were again. Those words *mercies* and *lovingkindness*. I had read them once before in the Jeremiah section of the Book. But I still couldn't understand what they meant. These were not words that I used every day. Loving and kindness were concepts I understood. I was starting to get that part. But *mercies* still escaped me. Once on the playground, a bully was holding Jimmy McDonald down and telling him to ask for mercy, to which Jimmy yelled, "Mercy!" The bully let Jimmy up, but retackled him when the boy tried to run. I was not getting the connection between the playground experience and this word used, at least twice I had seen, in the Bible. Jeanette would know. But just as soon as I had that thought, I realized how condescendingly I had looked at Jeanette and her misuse of everyday words. I felt ashamed and wanted to be forgiven for my thought and actions. Maybe I would get the courage to ask Jeanette to explain in a way that only she could what mercies were and how to see them new every day.

Camille made landfall on the Mississippi coast around midnight. I had managed half an hour of sleep before the usual nightmare ended it, and I awoke just in time to watch the eerie pictures being broadcast on TV. There was talk about the eye of the storm, the temporary calm that followed the initial fury of the hurricane. Newscasters said the back side of the storm was yet to come, and it would come with perhaps more rage than its front side. I got chills, which Jeanette had said was a sign that a rabbit was running over my grave.

The next two hours I slept again, missing the live reports of Camille's aftermath. When I awoke it was still dark outside and I was once again soaked in my own perspiration. I wanted to commit myself to sleeplessness, for I didn't want to experience another nightmare. I walked the halls of the hospital so I could have some rest from my own sleep.

The halls were empty and quiet. I listened for sounds of evacuees and emergency personnel who had been on call moving about, but there was no one. Even the nurse who had sat behind the large desk in the middle of the hall was not at her station.

I had a thought. I would try to go in and see Malcolm. If he was asleep, I wouldn't wake him. If he was awake, I would encourage him to remain silent and just let me hold his hand.

The double metal doors to the ICU were not locked. There was a sign on both doors that read No Admittance Hospital Personnel Only. I peeked through the window in one of the doors and saw no one on the hall. Perhaps if I was really quiet, I could slip into Malcolm's room without anyone knowing. I knew which room it was because I had seen Jeanette go in and out of that room several times over the past few days.

The door made a metallic groan as I first pushed it, but I kept pushing slowly. No alarm went off, and so I proceeded. I opened Malcolm's room door slightly and listened for the presence of a nurse. All I could hear was a high-pitched mechanical beep that I guessed was a monitor of Malcolm's heartbeat. I walked cautiously inside the room, listening for anything that might turn me away, but I heard nothing.

A large bed sat in the middle of the room. Machines surrounded it, flashing numbers that made no sense to me. A plastic tent covered the bed, but even through the almost opaque drape I could tell it was Malcolm. He was asleep. His face and his eyes looked swollen, but it was still the same face I was starting to cherish. I stood for a minute or two and just watched him. His chest rose and fell slowly, and his breathing was light and shallow. He was breathing, however. He was alive, and all I could do was say, "Thank you, God."

Malcolm's left hand had tubes taped to it, but his right hand was free of any restraint. I walked to the right side of the bed and reached under the tent. As I was about to take his hand, he raised it to meet mine. I expected Malcolm to open his eyes and smile. Just let me see you smile, I wished. But he didn't open his eyes nor smile. He just let his hand rest in mine, and that was enough.

Malcolm died before dawn.

Chapter Forty-two

It was my first funeral. There was crying, even sobbing. But there was laughter, too. Someone would remember something Malcolm had said or done, and then everyone would smile through the tears. Somehow it didn't seem inappropriate. Malcolm would have enjoyed it all.

The pastor stood in the pulpit over the flower-draped casket. "Today, Malcolm would have celebrated his seventeenth birthday," he began. Jeanette sniffed hard and loud. I would have, too, if I had had the strength. I just wiped the most recent tears from my cheeks.

The pastor paused and breathed deeply. "Malcolm was the most Christlike person I've ever known. He was selfless and innocent and willing to do whatever needed doing. Everybody knows how he cared for the roses out here in the back of the church." I hadn't known. "He made sure they got plenty of water and food, and when they got aphids, he tried to figure out the best way to protect the roses without harming the bugs." Everybody chuckled. "Malcolm didn't even want to hurt a bug." The pastor's voice started to crack, and he took another deep breath.

"But Malcolm was human, too. Once, a few years ago in Vacation Bible School, Malcolm couldn't get his popsicle sticks to stay glued together when he was trying make a pencil box. Finally, out of frustration, he hurled the whole thing across the room and then went and sat in a corner and pouted for a few minutes. We let him cool off, and before we knew it, he was picking up the sticks and gluing them together again."

I had never seen Malcolm hurl anything in anger nor pout, but I was glad he had not given up on his task. That was Malcolm, never wavering or giving up. I was living proof of that.

"Peace I leave with you, my peace I give unto you," the pastor read from a large Bible. "Not as the world giveth, give I unto you. Let not your heart be troubled, neither let it be afraid.

"Be careful for nothing; but in every thing by prayer and supplication with thanksgiving let your requests be made known unto God. And the peace of God, which passeth all understanding, shall keep your hearts and minds through Christ Jesus."

All I could think of was the haunting, annoying song about peace I had heard during my beach escape, "I've got peace like a river…," but I did not want to think of it, because I had no peace at all. When I gazed at the large bronze box in front of me that contained the lifeless body of my friend, all I could think of was the alternate words I had used once. "I've got rage like an ocean."

It wasn't fair. If Malcolm was so good and Christlike, why was he lying cold and dead before me? How could God do that?

The church was full. Overflowing. There were people sitting in folding chairs at the ends of the aisles and some standing around the perimeter of the room. I wondered briefly, if it had been me in the coffin, who would have come for my funeral. I assumed it would be held in the Methodist church in Jackson and that all my Alabama relatives would be there, but I was pretty certain my death wouldn't draw a standing-room-only crowd like that.

We filed out one row at a time, following the casket, which was carried by six men I didn't know.

At the cemetery I could better see the faces of those who had gathered around the casket to pay their respects. I recognized many of them. They had been the ones to come and go during the past few days. They had prayed, but why hadn't their prayers worked? If they were such religious people, why had God not done what they asked? They looked so sad and even surprised that their prayers had not been answered.

I said a silent good-bye to my friend and tried to keep myself from weeping as the graveside service ended. Turning my focus to the crowd one last time, I saw a face among the mourners I had not seen before. It was a woman who didn't look as though she belonged there. She was dressed in a cotton print skirt and white blouse. Both pieces of clothing looked too big for her. Her hair, which had equal amounts of brown and gray, was pulled back from her face into a ragged ponytail. She wore dingy sneakers and didn't carry a purse. She did have a handful of tissues that she used to dab the tears away from her eyes occasionally.

As the others moved slowly to their cars, the woman moved in the other direction, toward an opening in the wall surrounding the cemetery large enough for a person to walk through. She looked back one last time, and I was able to catch her eye. She smiled politely at me, and when she did, my heart skipped a beat. The smile was the same dimpled one I had seen so often on Malcolm's face. This had to be his mother.

"Here, dear." My grandmother opened her hand and produced a small yellow pill. Many of the mourners had congregated back at the beach house after the graveside service.

"What is this?" I asked, still surprised that my grandparents and my father had bothered to come to Malcolm's funeral at all.

"It's a Valium. You take it now. It'll calm you down and make you feel better."

I didn't want to feel better. I didn't want to calm down. I threw the pill in the toilet and was determined to feel whatever emotions I could conjure up. And I had an object upon which to focus my emotions— the woman I had seen at the cemetery. If she was who I thought she was, I didn't know what to feel about her. Anger? Pity?

The late August sun was relentless. Even when it finally would sink below the horizon, it hardly ever took its heat with it. There was nothing to do, day and night, but sit in our air-conditioned rooms and try to pass the time.

Jeanette hadn't had the courage yet to go into Malcolm's room, much less try to go through his personal things. I was sure the paper sack full of my hair was still in his top drawer, but I didn't care. Should someone find it, and they would eventually, I would claim it and, I imagined, have a good cry again. Until then, I would spend my remaining days at the colony working on the fragments of my summer experiences to see if I could make them fit into a whole picture.

"Mama, what do you know about Malcolm's parents?" I asked, venturing out on the screened-in porch early one morning while my mother was painting the rolling surf. Like the others, I could swear that her work was not only a convincing copy of the real thing, but if possible, it was even more beautiful.

My mother put down her brush and wiped her hands on a dish towel she had in her lap. She looked at me as if to chide me for asking. Malcolm's funeral had only been three days before, and so far no one had even mentioned his name. I was trying to understand the why of that, but I guessed it was too painful yet. I suddenly felt sorry for breaking that silence, and ashamed for broaching a subject that was even more heartbreaking: the abandonment of a mentally challenged boy.

She looked away for a moment "I don't know much about his parents, except that they left him here years ago, and Jeanette took him in and raised him as her own." And with that, my mother turned back to her painting. Her hand trembled as she lifted her brush, and I was certain then I had made a mistake in asking. Still, the question was out and I couldn't retract it. I decided to keep prodding.

"I saw a woman at the funeral." This made my mother's hand crush the paintbrush against the canvas, leaving an ugly stain in a place I was sure she hadn't intended it to be.

Mama opened her mouth, but controlled the curse word that was trying to form on her lips.

The damage had been done, so I ventured to finish my thought. "She had Malcolm's dimple."

My mother sat there awhile, staring at her ruined seascape. I braced myself for a tongue-lashing, which I deserved. Instead, she finally looked at me and said, "I saw her, too."

I welcomed the silent thought I shared with my mother. It served as a distraction from the sorrow, the boredom, the heat, the dread. I still had no definitive answer about what would happen after the summer was officially over. My father had already returned to Jackson with my grandparents, but his good-bye was not particularly emotional, nor did it sound the least bit final. I figured that meant something, but I had no idea what.

Mary Alice Spaulding took over the cooking duties for the few days after Malcolm's death. She explained to us that she wanted to give Jeanette time to rest and grieve. Though I didn't say anything, I figured Jeanette hadn't really wanted the time off, that she would rather stay busy. However, in such matters, I had learned not to question the decisions of the adults in charge. After a couple of days of Mrs. Spaulding's cooking, those of us who remained—Mama, me, and Jeanette—had had enough.

"Cornbread needs more salt," Jeanette said as tactfully as Jeanette could say anything.

Mrs. Spaulding's shoulders drooped. She shook her head slightly. "I'm sorry, Jeanette. Nobody makes pone like you, honey." I had noticed the return of Mary Alice Spaulding's Southernness since she had been with us. Her Deep South accent had apparently been hiding somewhere beneath her sophistication and had only needed a few weeks around Jeanette for it to resurface.

"I think it's okay," I said, trying to help everybody's feelings but silently agreeing with Jeanette. I hoped my little white lie wouldn't keep Jeanette away from the stove. I hoped, too, that my mother wouldn't volunteer for kitchen duty. All of my life we had existed on canned soups, frozen pizzas, and tacos. When friends of mine would come to my house for sleepovers, it had always seemed to them a treat. They would always explain that they never got to eat such fun food. Their tables had always been set with fresh vegetables, fried meats, and sweet tea; and that had been another way in which I was different.

Chapter Forty-three

D addy called," my mother announced as I walked into the cabin. I had decided to brave the heat and humidity one afternoon to walk the beach, not toward the Hangout, but in the opposite direction. I wanted to find the exact place I had drifted to, the exact spot at which Malcolm had entered the gulf to rescue me. Not totally sure I was at the right place, but certain I was pretty close, I sat at the water's edge and wept for Malcolm. I knew he would be mad at me for crying for him, but I could do nothing else. I missed him, I wanted him alive again, I was angry at him for trying to swim out to me that day. Why had he tried such a crazy stunt? Why had I? Why hadn't he waited until rescuers came? Why had he been there at all? I should have been swept out to sea. I should have drowned. I should have died. The depth of my grief, my shame, my anger made me want to hurl myself back into the gulf, yet it seemed as though an invisible force held me down on the sand. After a while, I was able to move again, to walk again, and I found myself back at the cabin hearing the news.

"We're going home next week." Mama said, looking at me intently, I guessed to try to read my reaction.

"Back to Jackson?" That place I had lived all my life suddenly didn't feel like home anymore.

"Yeah," Mama answered. "School starts back before Labor Day this year, and we need to get you ready."

"What do you mean, 'ready'?" I asked.

"Clothes mostly. You've grown so much this summer, I'm sure none of your school clothes will fit this year."

I had realized I was taller and slightly rounder since I had come to Florida, but it hadn't dawned on me how much. I glanced over into the full-length mirror in the main room and almost didn't recognize the girl I saw. My legs were longer, but still somewhat shapeless. My arms, bronzed from the sun, were proportionately thicker. My face was rounder, too, but I wasn't sure if it was from gaining weight or from the short haircut I had been sporting those last few weeks. The layers had grown out fairly evenly by now, and I was able to create a pin curl over each ear. The hair was long enough, too, that a bobby pin would hold a velvet bow in place on the right side.

"Mama, I don't want to go." I was surprised I had said it, though I had felt it for some time.

"What?" my mother asked, though she didn't sound too surprised.

"I'm not sure I want to go back to Jackson."

My mother moved toward me and stood looking at me as I looked at myself in the mirror. She slid her hands around my waist and cocked her head to one side so I could see her face in the mirror. She rested her head on my shoulder, and for a moment we looked like a two-headed creature. I noticed how similar our faces were.

She sighed. "I know. I think I feel the same way."

"But…" I raised an eyebrow.

"But…we have to go home sometime."

She unwrapped her arms from around me and turned to walk away.

"I hate Daddy." It wasn't just a passing comment and it wasn't accidental either. It was deliberate and honest.

I could see her still in the mirror, and when she turned back to me, she looked more hurt than angry. "Kat, honey, you can't say that."

"Why not? I don't think he cares about us so much."

I turned around and faced my mother. Her eyes looked up as though searching for the right words in her brain, but if she found them, she did not speak them. Instead, she silently walked to the leather couch and sat down. I followed and sat with her silently for, it seemed like, ten minutes.

Finally she spoke. "Do you think we ought to look for Malcolm's mother?"

Though I was sure this was a diversion to keep us from talking about the statement of contempt I had just made about my father, I was startled to hear her ask such a question. Ever since I had seen the woman with Malcolm's dimple at the funeral, I was intrigued by the same thought: Should we look for the woman we suspected to be Malcolm's biological mother? And if so, why?

"Have you mentioned it to Mrs. Spaulding or Jeanette yet?"

"No."

"Think we ought to?" I asked.

"I would hate to upset Jeanette. She's already been through so much," she said. I nodded. "But I thought I might ask Mary Alice."

Jeanette announced at breakfast that she would be resuming the cooking duties again. She announced it just as she was about to bite into a too-crisp link of sausage. If Mary Alice Spaulding had ever been a good cook, she had apparently fallen out of practice. Almost everything we had eaten over the past few days was overcooked, under-salted, or missing a key ingredient. I figured a lady like Mrs. Spaulding had, indeed, not cooked for a while. I guessed someone of her stature had hired servants to prepare meals. I was glad, however, that we would not have to endure more of her unsavory meals.

"Okay, then. But let me keep the cleanup duty," Mrs. Spaulding added.

There was an inaudible collective sigh from the rest of us. "Kat and I will help," Mama chimed in. Ordinarily, I would have been annoyed at being volunteered for anything, but I was starting to feel that I needed to help out more.

We stacked the breakfast dishes on the counter near the sink. "Kat, can you unload the dishwasher?" Mama asked. Jeanette was about to retreat to her bedroom when my mother pulled Mrs. Spaulding aside. They were within earshot, and I listened intently as I put the clean dishes in the cabinets.

"Mary Alice, what do you know about Malcolm's mother?" my mother asked.

Mrs. Spaulding turned and looked at Mama. Glancing toward Jeanette's room, she finally answered. "Why do you ask?"

After a quick look at me, my mother continued, "Well, Kat and I saw a woman at the funeral...."

Mrs. Spaulding interjected, "Vera."

I almost dropped a plate. I stepped closer to the women and whispered, "Who?"

"Malcolm's mother," Mrs. Spaulding said.

My mother took over. "You mean you know her?" Mama looked at me and motioned at me with her hand to keep at my task.

"Well, I know of her."

"Does Jeanette know?" I couldn't help but ask, interrupting my chore once again to get closer to the conversation.

"No. Only I know." Mrs. Spaulding paused and looked at us. "Now you know, I guess."

"We don't know anything, really," Mama said. "We saw a woman at the funeral that could have been Malcolm's mother. We're just guessing."

Mrs. Spaulding reached for a clean glass on the top rack of the dishwasher. She pushed it into my mother's hand before she reached for the refrigerator handle. Opening the door, Mary Alice pulled a pitcher of cold lemonade from the top shelf and filled the glass my mother was holding. She took the glass from my mother's hand and took a long, cool drink. Looking toward Jeanette's closed door, she finally said, "It's a long story. Let's talk later."

The curiosity was killing me. All through lunch, I was so anxious to hear the story of Vera and Malcolm that I almost blurted out the question in front of everybody. I managed to restrain myself, but while I was helping clear the lunch plates from the table, I found myself getting slightly annoyed that Jeanette didn't disappear soon enough. I hoped Mrs. Spaulding wouldn't keep us in suspense until nightfall.

I was delighted to hear Jeanette announce, "I'm gonna make a run to the groc'ry here in a minute. We need milk and eggs and"—she stopped suddenly—"y'all want anything?" The three of us shook our heads, and I tried futilely to think of something to keep Jeanette away from the house longer.

After gathering her purse and keys, Jeanette walked out the carport door. When we heard her car crank up and pull out of the driveway, Mrs. Spaulding, my mother, and I huddled in front of the kitchen sink.

"Vera and James Kent," Mrs. Spaulding began. "Those were Malcolm's biological parents." She looked at me as if wondering whether I understood the term *biological*. I nodded my head.

"They were from up in Michigan someplace. I had an application from Vera, under a different name, a couple of times for grants into one of our colonies."

"She's an artist?" my mother asked.

"Yes. She'd been accepted into a couple of programs as Sara McKinney. I only knew her through her applications and by her work."

"What kind of work did she do?" Only my mother would have asked it.

"Charcoals. Oils. Other media, too." Mrs. Spaulding painted an imaginary stroke with her finger. "She's talented."

"What does this have to do with Malcolm?" I pressed.

"Well, nothing I guess, except it brought Vera, or Sara, here many summers ago."

"Was that the summer she left Malcolm?" my mother asked. I was glad she at least was back on the important subject.

"Yes. She had James with her, too."

"James?" I asked.

"Malcolm's father," she answered.

"Oh yeah," I remembered out loud.

"But that's not the name he gave us, of course. He was Jack McKinney then," Mrs. Spaulding added.

"What?" my mother crossed her arms in front of her and leaned forward.

Mrs. Spaulding looked a little confused herself. Then she shook her head. "Okay, let me start over."

∞

Chapter Forty-Four

The large hand-carved wooden box looked expensive, exotic, as though it had come from the Far East. The wood smelled like cedar, but not as pungent. Its sweet aroma got stronger as Mary Alice Spaulding opened the lid and revealed the box's contents.

There were several papers and clippings encased in plastic. Others were pressed neatly between pieces of cardboard, which were taped together. Mrs. Spaulding pulled one of those out of the box and carefully un-taped the cardboard sides. Between them was a slightly wrinkled piece of paper that she gently handed to my mother. Mama gasped and pulled the page closer to her to study its contents.

"What is it?" I asked. I didn't want to grab at the page since it seemed to be something of value. My mother slowly handed me the paper while still holding a look of astonishment on her face.

I gasped, too, but I followed it with a well of tears in my eyes.

"It's Malcolm," I finally managed to say.

It was, indeed, a charcoal drawing of an impish Malcolm at maybe two years old. Even in black charcoal, the resemblance was uncanny. The wisp of baby hair was captured in thin, delicate lines. His round face radiated sweetness, and the dimple was undeniable.

"His mother...Vera...drew this?" my mother asked.

"Yes." Mrs. Spaulding lifted out another page protected by heavy cardboard.

For the following few minutes, we three sat in silence and looked at the drawings and small paintings that Mrs. Spaulding pulled from the box. Even I could recognize the genius of the artist, but I was more intrigued with and touched by the beauty of the face the works depicted. They were all Malcolm at various stages of young childhood.

As a newborn, an infant, a toddler. However, there didn't seem to be any pictures of him past the age of five or so. I remembered Jeanette telling my mother that Malcolm had been about five when he had been left with her at the colony.

"A few years ago, I got a letter from Vera."

Mama and I stopped looking at the pictures and focused on the gentle face of Mary Alice Spaulding as she told the story. "Of course, I knew about Malcolm. Jeanette told me all about it. She even told me about his parents, their names...well, the names they gave her, any-way...and about how she decided to unofficially adopt him. I was glad these two had found each other, even if in unusual circumstances.

"I was not, however, in favor of Jeanette's refusal to call the authori-ties. I didn't want her to get in trouble later. Who knows what the legal system might have done to her should the parents have returned? They could have charged her with kidnapping, all kinds of things, so I encour-aged her to call the police. She would not."

I glanced, out the window, hoping Jeanette was taking her time at the store.

"Yes, Jeanette told me the same thing, Mary Alice," Mama said. "It was like she was willing to take whatever legal heat she might get just so she could protect Malcolm from his abusive parents."

"Abusive father," Mrs. Spaulding corrected. She then described James with synonyms for *evil* until she ran out of words.

My inklings had apparently been right. I had imagined Malcolm's mother loved him. And I had believed his father to be the way Mrs. Spaulding was describing.

"That's how I came into possession of these drawings and such."

I wasn't following. But she continued. "About five years ago, I got a letter and this picture in the mail." Mrs. Spaulding held up the first pic-ture she had shown us of Malcolm as a toddler. "The letter was from Vera. I didn't recognize the name at first because she had applied to my colonies under another name, but she told me her story. By the picture and by her description of the events surrounding the abandonment, I knew she was Malcolm's mother. She confessed to everything and begged my forgiveness.

"She explained that her husband had recently been sent to prison for murder. She said she had always been afraid to divorce him, but with him in prison, she at last felt safe enough to contact me.

"After that, she hopped a bus and came down to Panama City where she had left Malcolm."

I asked, "To get him back?" I couldn't imagine the audacity of that.

"No," Mrs. Spaulding explained. "She just wanted to see if he was all right."

"That still doesn't explain why she contacted you," my mother said.

"Well, apparently after she was sure Malcolm was still here and being cared for so well, she didn't want to upset him or Jeanette. But she somehow wanted to make up for her actions years before." Mrs. Spaulding repositioned herself on the leather couch. "She knew how to get in touch with me because of the times she had applied to my colonies. She sent me a check for fifty dollars and asked if I would make sure it got to Malcolm without him or Jeanette knowing about it. In fact, every month after that, she sent me fifty dollars."

"What did you do with it?" I asked. Doing the math in my head, I realized that fifty dollars a month over five years would be a significant amount of money.

"Well, I wanted to put it in a trust fund for Malcolm, but Vera wanted Malcolm to have it then, so I increased Jeanette's allowance by fifty dollars starting that month. She never knew why, and I knew she'd spend it on things he needed."

"Is Malcolm's father still in prison?" I asked. I hoped he was and that he would never hurt anyone again.

"No," Mrs. Spaulding answered. "James died in prison less than a year ago. Vera sent the obituary that appeared in the paper," she added, handing me a newspaper clipping. There was a grainy black-and-white picture of the man, who, I was happy to note, didn't look like Malcolm at all. I also noticed there was only one person on his list of survivors.

Vera's name was given as his ex-wife. No parents or siblings. No mention of Malcolm at all.

I recalled the conversation I had overheard between Jeanette and my mother and how Malcolm's birth certificate could not be found. And then, looking again at the obituary, I realized that it was as if he had never existed.

"So was Malcolm's real last name Kent?" I asked.

"Yes. Vera and James had given an alias to Jeanette, you know, so they couldn't be traced. That's why Jeanette couldn't find a birth certificate for Malcolm. Maybe she and James had been planning this...abandonment...for several years. Maybe it took a while for Vera to find a suitable place to leave little Malcolm. I guess that says something for the love of a mother and the integrity of Jeanette."

My mother hadn't said anything in a while. Apparently she had been taking it all in. "Have you met with this Vera, Mary Alice?" I detected some animosity in my mother's reference to "this Vera."

"No, I haven't."

"Do you think Jeanette saw her at the funeral?" I asked.

"I don't know. Mary Alice slowly ran her fingers through her hair and then shook her head. "She hasn't said anything to me."

Chapter Forty-five

W e only had a few days left at the colony and one morning I awoke with a sense of panic.

It wasn't because of all the things that had to be done before we headed for home. It wouldn't take me too long to pack. Most of my things were still in the suitcases my grandmother had brought to the hospital, when we'd refused our forced exodus. Mama's art supplies, canvases, and watercolors she had painted over the past three months, however, had grown in quantity, but I believed it all could be loaded quickly and carried home easily.

It wasn't the packing, then, that gave me a feeling of urgency and dread. It had to be something else. There was some unfinished business left for me to do, although I wasn't sure what it was.

The clock said 7:15. Without looking, I knew the other women in the house were already up and going about their usual routines.

My mother would be sitting out on the dune with a cup of coffee, basking in the morning light and trying to conjure up some last-minute inspiration for her canvas.

Jeanette was already puttering around the kitchen, maybe even starting to cook breakfast.

Mary Alice Spaulding would be sitting at the small desk in her room, reading the newspaper or writing letters. Though I had not risen early many times, I had seen the new light of morning enough to know that everyone in the cabin had her own way of getting ready to face another day.

"Good morning, Jeanette," I said, finding her exactly where I had expected, laying strips of bacon side by side in a frying pan.

"Mornin', shug," she answered back. I could tell she was starting to feel a little more normal with each day that passed. We all missed Malcolm terribly, but the shock we had felt was melting into quiet sorrow and into a realization that he wouldn't be coming to our table anymore.

"Smells good," I commented, realizing this was one of the few times I had ever risen early enough for a hot breakfast and maybe the first time I had ever complimented Jeanette on anything.

"Thank ya. It'll be ready directly." Jeanette abandoned the frying pan long enough to fetch a pitcher of orange juice from the refrigerator and pour some into a glass for me.

"I…uh, thank you, Jeanette."

For the next few minutes, I studied my surroundings while I sipped the orange juice. I was trying to take it all in since I would be leaving it soon.

The white porcelain stove behind where Jeanette was standing looked like an antique, but if its age had made it less functional, no one could tell. The biscuits and the pot roasts that came out of the oven had been perfectly delicious. The refrigerator, which Jeanette called "the Fridg'daire," hummed along beautifully, keeping everything put into it cold even though I had heard Jeanette say that both of the appliances had come over on the ark. When I had asked why Mrs. Spaulding didn't replace them for the colony, Jeanette had replied, "Land sakes, chile. You don't toss sumpin' out just 'cause it's old. These here appliances is almost like family to me." I remembered rolling my eyes at that statement, but at that moment I could see Jeanette's reasoning. She maneuvered around the small L-shaped space with such familiarity that her moves were almost graceful.

I rubbed my hand over the surface of the long wooden table where I was seated as though to say farewell. Farewell to the meals, the conversations, and the people who had sat there. Malcolm had liked to sit on the end of the bench nearest the sink. I had started sitting on the opposite end of the table, but on the same side of the bench. That way, I could eat in peace without Malcolm watching my every bite. The times

I had sat across the table from him, I had caught him opening his mouth at the same time I was forking food into mine. Those times I had left the table in disgust, and at the next meals, I had made sure I was out of Malcolm's line of sight.

I stared into my empty glass and ached to see his gaze once more. It was then that I looked toward his room. Every day before that one, his door had been closed. This time it stood open.

I gasped.

"What?" Jeanette asked, looking back at me suddenly.

I wanted to say nothing, but apparently my eyes were still glued to Malcolm's open door, and Jeanette knew immediately what I meant.

"Yeah," she began. "Couldn't sleep last night, so I figured I'd clean his room."

I dreaded to hear what she had found that had once belonged to me. Before I could ask, Jeanette turned and looked at me.

"I saved it for you," she said. I was pretty sure I knew "it" meant the sack full of my hair I had once discarded. I blushed. Then I felt tears sting my eyes. Was it shame for my rebellion? Was it grief for my friend? Either way, I couldn't force myself to look Jeanette Hudspeth in the eye. Fortunately, she didn't require it. Instead she walked around the table, wrapped her soft, thick arm around my head, and pulled me close to her body. She didn't speak at all, but just let me weep for a moment.

"The bacon needs turnin'," she said finally. She pulled away, and I felt like I wanted to follow her to beg for forgiveness, compassion, and wisdom.

Over the past two days, I had noticed Jeanette starting to talk to herself again, a good sign that she was healing, if slowly. But as she turned the bacon in the frying pan, her singing—which had once annoyed me vigorously—returned as well. She had often hummed or sang as she cooked and cleaned, mostly songs I had never heard. Many of them had been about God, but the words she sang had never made sense to me. This time, however, the words were not only familiar; they were haunting.

"Great is thy faithfulness! Great is thy faithfulness. Morning by morning new mercies I see."

I suddenly remembered an earlier vow I had made: to find "new mercies" I had read about in my secondhand Bible.

Chapter Forty-six

A fter breakfast, I sat at the table, waiting for some cosmic cue. The kitchen was empty now and I felt at ease sorting through my thoughts.

Vera. Vera. I let the name roll over in my head a few times, thinking it would help me conjure up an image of what she would be like holding Malcolm as a baby. Vera. The name seemed old-fashioned for the woman I had seen briefly at the graveside service.

Finally, I moved. I stepped out on the back porch and scanned the horizon for something…anything to take my mind off of my sudden, unfounded anxiety. Was there something I still needed to do? Unspoken feelings to my mother? Tears yet to be shed for Malcolm? Questions I still needed to ask about Vera?

Somewhere in the back of my mind, my decision to learn about mercies hovered, but I didn't know where to begin.

From the corner of my eye, I saw my mother emerging from her morning dune time, and as she walked toward the surf instead of the house, I was safe to watch her for a while.

The summer had taken its toll on my mother. She had never seemed old to me before, but suddenly I noticed she was at least looking her age. Thirty-three maybe? Thirty-four? I was embarrassed that I didn't know her exact age. But I was glad I had started to develop a more grown-up rapport with her, and I felt the pangs of hunger to know more.

It didn't take long for Mama to soak in the morning and then come back to her easel to spill it onto a canvas or a piece of paper.

I took a few minutes to dress for the day, giving her time to settle into her work. I also wanted to give her time to get into a new image. I wanted to see what she had seen. I could tell, even from a distance, there was something incredible coming out of the end of her paintbrush. I hesitated a few minutes longer, waiting for her mind to take a breath before I joined her on the porch. Before I approached her, I stopped and filled a mug of coffee that I would present to her.

"Thanks, hon," my mother said as she accepted the hot mug from me. Her tone of voice indicated she was much more chipper than me. Apparently she didn't share my feeling of foreboding.

"You're welcome." I sat down on the cot next to her easel. "So? What do you think about this whole thing with Vera?"

I had read my mother's mood wrong. Before I had time to tuck my feet under me and lean over on one elbow, she began to unleash her thoughts. "I don't get it. I just don't get it. How selfish can one be?"

I didn't know whom she was labeling selfish—Vera or Jeanette. It could have gone either way. I couldn't contribute to the conversation until I had cleared that question up.

"Who's selfish?" I asked.

My mother suddenly turned to me with a look of surprise. It was as if she had just noticed I was there. Then there was a look of embarrassment on her face as if she hadn't intended for me to hear what she was thinking.

I tried to explain my question. "Well, I mean, I'm not sure who's the most, you know, selfish in all this."

"Children shouldn't be passed around like a pet dog or something. 'Here, you feed him, no, you feed him.'"

I had never had a pet, so I wasn't as emotionally involved in Mama's analogy as perhaps she would have liked.

"I don't get it." I sat up and hung my legs over the side of the cot. When I did, my mother and I were facing each other, almost touching, knee to knee.

"You don't get what?"

"Well, I mean, since when did you start thinking about what's best for a child?" I immediately clamped my hand over my mouth. I had spoken honestly, but insolently. That had been, however, the unsettling question that had just come to the surface.

I must have cast my eyes downward for a split second, because I didn't see my mother's hand approach my face until after the sting of it reached my nerve endings.

My mother gasped at the same time I did. Before I could react, either with tears or with a reciprocal slap, her arms were around my shoulders, and she was squeezing me tightly as she let go of the sobs from her throat.

I couldn't cry. My senses and emotions hadn't kept up with the still-fresh shock of her reaction. My mother had never struck me, even when I was a child, and so this incongruous gesture was too fresh to comprehend.

"I'm so sorry." My mother's sobs muffled her words, but I understood them perfectly. It had been a long time since I had seen my mother cry this way. In fact, I couldn't remember the last time. She had shed silent tears at Malcolm's funeral, but I had never seen her truly weep. Nor did I ever remember her holding me so tightly. It was as if she had been waiting for an appropriate time to let all of her sorrow go.

Finally, she pulled away. Her face was swollen and splotchy, and she winced as if she were in pain.

"Mama?" I couldn't take my eyes off of her. I had gone from shocked to incensed to concerned. Just as I was silently vowing to never bring up the subject again, she regained some composure.

"Do you think I don't care about you or something?" She was almost childlike.

"I, uh, don't…"

"Is that what you think?" Her tone was starting to sound a bit riled.

"No." I mustered some courage. "I mean, yeah, sometimes I wonder."

That was all it took. In the hour or so that followed, I felt free for the first time to tell my mother how neglected I had felt…what a sense of dismissal I had harbored for so long. My mother's mahogany-colored eyes stayed focused on me as I tried to express the feelings of misplacement I'd had for as long as I could remember feeling anything. She didn't rebuke me nor interrupt except to ask questions now and again.

I told her how it felt looking different from my Aryan relatives, how I felt like an old rag doll being dragged around by her creative whims, how I felt Daddy was choosing his parents over us.

I had never loved my mother so much, and I had never felt so grown-up. Miraculously, we were left alone on that August morning to talk honestly, on equal ground, until we both finally wound down and were without anything left to say.

I'd had a glimpse of what new mercies were about.

And it was like cleaning out my toy chest. I took items inside me and laid each one out to evaluate. I reminisced for a while with some feelings. Then I had to decide to keep the ones that still brought me joy and discard those I had outgrown. And as with the older toys, I had moments of sadness and even regret as I forced myself to abandon the more childish thoughts.

Chapter Forty-seven

I didn't cry when we drove away. Neither did my mother. Jeanette did a little, and so did Mrs. Spaulding. But I wondered if their tears could have been more from relief that we were leaving. I could imagine them wanting to be alone to continue sorting out their sorrows. Maybe they would talk about Vera. Maybe Mary Alice would show Jeanette the box with Malcolm's pictures in it. Maybe Jeanette would be surprised. Maybe not. And maybe Jeanette would try to connect with Vera and share their burdens. I hoped Jeanette would tell Vera about looking for new mercies, and that Vera would be watching for them as I had the past few days.

I started to see mercy as we turned north, leaving the gulf and the sand, the people and their influence, where we had found them just a few months before. I glanced over at my mother as she drove. She apparently was lost in thought, for she didn't return my gaze, and so I kept my eyes on her for a while.

The hum of the car was soothing and allowed my mind to think deeper than usual. I started drawing a picture in my head of the perfect mother. I used parts from the three mothers I had observed over that summer. One, my own, loving me without a doubt, but still struggling with her sense of duty, her free spirit, her fading dreams. I used my image of Jeanette, the surrogate, in her being Malcolm's ultimate provider. Then there was Vera. I was still trying to find her in my head, and I could only wonder who she was. She'd had no sense of duty, no need to provide, yet somehow had become a supreme protector of her child. She had left her son for his own good and then returned to try to watch over him from a distance like a guardian angel. What pain all three of these women had suffered. What love they had, a love so deep that sacrifice was a given.

Epilogue

s soon as the plane climbs to ten thousand feet, the illuminated Fasten Seat Belt sign goes dark, and an announcement says we can move about the cabin. The warning, however, is to keep our seat belts fastened while seated in case of turbulence. I thumb my nose at the turbulence and unlatch my seat beat.

I reach for my carry-on bag stuffed under the seat in front of me. As I unzip the top, a musty aroma hits my senses. I have to dig only a little while to find the source of the smell…my Bible, which still retains the faint odor of old coffee grounds from that summer when I threw it away and Malcolm retrieved it for me from the kitchen garbage can. It is more weathered than ever, pages stained and marked; the cover brittle and bent. I open it. It always summons me, every time a reminder of my watercolor summer when stains on the rag paper of my life became clear, even beautiful. A masterpiece. It was because of these horrible events that I learned about faith, accepted grace and forgiveness. And these lessons became more valuable to me as the years moved on. For many years now I have been a child of the Master Artist.

My father and my mother never reconciled. Instead, they went back to living parallel lives for a while but never tried to connect again. The fall after I graduated from high school, my mother packed her things and moved to Baltimore, where she paints, shows her work, and lives…alone.

I'm still my Daddy's Bee-bee even though I'm grown with a family of my own. My father got married again to a nice woman, a woman he had dated in high school and who had her own version of marital disappointments. They seem to be happy in the house I grew up in.

A bookmark slides out from between the pages of the Bible. I silently vow to unclutter this book someday. Too many clippings and notes stress the binding of this already well-worn Book. I promise, however, never to discard the slippery bookmark. It's torn and faded, a single strip of paper that I laminated to protect. Now even the plastic coating is showing too much wear. It has a boy's name on it in a child's handwriting. Malcolm. And it has a Scripture verse written underneath the name; a reference I put there before I sealed it from the elements. Jeremiah 31:3.

I fan the pages under my thumb and let the Book open naturally to the words.

Hear me, O LORD; for thy lovingkindness is good:
turn unto me according to the multitude of thy tender mercies.

As usual, I try to take one or two words from this prayer of the prophet and see what new thing I can glean from them. *Tender mercies* is my choice for today. I lean back in my seat and hear the sound of a baby crying in the seat in front me and feel the thump of a child behind me kicking my seat. Yes. Tender mercies. It's not so profound as it is comforting. It is my prayer for today.